The DREAM KEEPER

The
DREAM KEEPER

Margery Evernden

Lothrop, Lee & Shepard Books   New York

Printed in the United States of America.

First Edition

1 2 3 4 5 6 7 8 9 10

Designed by Sheila Lynch

Library of Congress Cataloging in Publication Data

Evernden, Margery.
   The dream keeper.

   Summary: Her parents' impending separation leads a
gifted thirteen-year-old musician to discover the story of
her great-grandmother's immigration to America from a
Jewish shtetl in Poland.
   [1. Grandmothers—Fiction.   2. Jews—Poland—Fiction.
3. Jews—United States—Fiction.   4. Family problems—
Fiction]   I. Title.
PZ7.E922Hap   1985   [Fic]   85–88
ISBN 0–688–04638–X

ALSO BY MARGERY EVERNDEN

The Kite Song

In Memory of
Mary Carbolofsky, Christian Gulbrandsen,
and the uncounted brave children of many
races and creeds who have followed their
dreams across the seas to America

Contents

Part One

Becka ∽

A two-day-old snow lay deep on the front yards of the tall brick houses on St. James Place. It rose in icy, rough-sculpted hedges beside the shoveled sidewalks. Even here, inside her great-grandmother's snug, second-story bedroom where Becka came every afternoon after school, veins of ice flashed in rainbow hues on the panes of the broad bay window. Becka herself sank into the familiar, chintz-covered wing chair, still shivering from the February cold outside—shivering also with an uneasiness that would not let her rest.

She gazed toward the big brass bed. One thing, at least, was certain. Bobe would not rise to claim the wing chair, since she had been confined for weeks to that bed beside the window. Judith and Patrick, Becka's mother and father—both of them sternly devoted to the use of first names between parents and children—had placed the bed so that the frail old woman could see the sky, the trees, and the faces of the houses across the street.

Despite their care Bobe seldom appeared to look outward nowadays. She simply lay upon her back, a ripple under the thick down comforter. Her head was as bony as that of some ancient bird, her white hair a feathery floss falling upon her pillow. Much of the time, the lids that guarded her fierce, sunken eyes were closed or, at the most, faintly fluttering.

All at once, as Becka leaned forward, those old eyes opened and looked directly at her. Becka spoke first.

"I just got home. I must have wakened you, Bobe."

"Yes, you did, girl. I was dreaming. I was always a great dreamer, you know." The old woman's answer was surprisingly strong and clear. "Don't you have dreams?"

"Well, y-yes. Yes, I do. Only, I mostly forget them as soon as I wake up."

"I never did that." Bobe shook her snowy head. "I never forgot one. After my mama died, I went to bed early every night so that I could dream she was alive again. For a long time, my dreams were the best part of my life. That was how I found my brother Aaron, you know, when he'd been taken away to the Tsar's army."

It was the longest speech Bobe had made in weeks, and it was doubly startling since she rarely mentioned her childhood. Becka leaned still closer to encourage the flow of words.

"You say you found Aaron, Bobe?"

"Yes, my oldest brother. The violinist. The one I used to love so much, more even than my sister Rachel or Papa or any of the others except, of course, Mama." Becka saw the old woman's shrunken left hand, with its disfigured index finger, twitch indignantly beneath the covers. "Where do you think you got your musical gift, girl? Not from your father, surely. And not from my papa. He was tone-deaf, poor man. Your great-grandpa Eric was only a little better, even though he was so clever in other ways. No, the gift came from Aaron and my mama's family. Your mother has told you about Aaron?"

"Yes. She says I should be very proud." Becka glanced toward the faded poster upon the wall beside the bed.

Bobe's sharp eyes followed her gaze.

"That was the announcement of Aaron's Carnegie Music Hall debut in New York City, you know."

"When was that concert, Bobe?"

"In 1916 . . . nineteen hundred and sixteen. Many long years ago. . . . I never thought that I would live so long. . . ."

And at that moment, with the world tipping like an egg timer, so that time past and time present seemed hardly more than a matter of whether you stood upon your head or your feet, Becka heard her father letting himself in at the front door downstairs. It had to be he, so meticulously bolting the door behind him. Despite Patrick's frequent warnings that even in Shadyside there could be break-ins, Judith rarely bothered with locks.

Starting guiltily, Becka remembered her father's other and often-repeated admonition. "We must all be very careful not to overtax Bobe's strength." And indeed, the old woman seemed already to have grown weary, her eyelids fluttering, moth-pale.

Hastily Becka leaped up from the chair. There was no time to go down the hall to her own room, undetected, to get her violin and the music that could always soothe Bobe into peaceful sleep.

"I'll play something on the tape recorder," she offered quickly. "The Brahms sonata, violin and piano? You always love Brahms."

Mercifully, Patrick seemed to linger longer than usual downstairs. By the time he had climbed the wide sweep of steps, Becka had found the Brahms cassette, whisked it into the recorder on the night table beside Bobe's bed, and snapped the black button. Music was pouring across the bedroom in a soft stream of sound as Patrick looked in upon them and then wordlessly turned back toward his and Judith's room.

"You shouldn't have done that, girl." Bobe sighed reprovingly and shook her head upon the pillow. "Poor Patrick. He didn't dare interrupt us. He is lonely in this house."

It was a disturbing thing to say, stabbing at Becka's own secret fears. "Don't try to talk anymore, Bobe," she whispered anxiously. "Just listen. Listen to the music."

But, shaking her head, the old woman went on as if borne upon a sudden new surge of strength.

"Let me say this, girl. I've thought about it all so long. I must talk now. The truth is, I sometimes wonder whether you and your parents should have come here to live with me last year. It seemed such a good idea at the time, with your grandpa Berkowitz retiring and moving to Florida. Your mother had been so restless living in that crowded little duplex and doing all her own housework. She hadn't been brought up that way, you know. Besides, there were so many advantages for us all here. You could have a lovely big room, live close to your music teacher, and go to Winchester, your mother's old school. Your father would be nearer his law office and could take over Grandpa Berkowitz's study. Your mother could use the living room for rehearsals. And I could stay in my own home. No one guessed then, of course, that I would

have such a stupid stroke. . . . No one guessed so many things.
. . . Oh, I have wondered. . . ."

Then Bobe's words faded, becoming so faint that Becka
could no longer hear them above the surging music. The tiny
old body, after its brief strength, was failing. The fierce eyes
were closing tight. Bobe was, after all, giving herself up to the
sounds. It was only when the sonata ended and the tape clicked
to its close that she spoke again, this time as if from somewhere
far away.

"Follow your father, girl. He's gone back downstairs. Go
now. Speak to him."

Throat tightening, Becka slipped to the stairway landing.
Despite her frailty, Bobe had heard sharply, as always. Patrick
was already at the door in the hall below, his back turned to
her. Set beside him, in the sparkle of light reflected from the
fanlight above the door, were his suitcase, a great stubby pair
of orange boots, and, propped against the wall, a pair of skis.

She knew in that instant that she would not, could not
speak to him. His thoughts were far from her. Swiftly she
stepped back into the shadows of the upper hall, back to the
doorway of her own bedroom.

"After all," she whispered passionately to herself, "I
should not be surprised."

Becka had had other troubles this winter, of course. As Bobe
often said, in this world no foot escapes blisters; pebbles slip
into every shoe. She must learn to ignore small hurts: some of
the girls at Winchester who were open-mouthed, even mock-
ing because of the long hours she spent practicing her violin;

the teachers, most of whom seemed to think their special subjects—social studies or mathematics or French—were more important than anything else, more important certainly than music. Such hurts died away. This season's brooding uneasiness had been something altogether different.

"Could be our age," Ginny Witherspoon, her best friend, had suggested cheerily whenever Becka sighed.

Yet surely, Becka thought, being thirteen—or, for that matter, three or thirty—had nothing to do with this unaccustomed sadness. The truth, unconfessed even to Ginny, was that her turmoil must reflect some problem lurking within the O'Brien family.

If there was nothing wrong, why had Mrs. Capek, Bobe's longtime housekeeper, taken to scowling disapprovingly as she propelled her vacuum cleaner and mop through the big, high-ceilinged rooms? Why did her father and mother so often pass each other without speaking? Why did Patrick no longer interrupt Judith's practicing, not even to drop a kiss upon her head? Why were their voices so mysteriously hushed behind their bedroom door at night? Why, on some nights when Becka was climbing into bed, had Patrick not yet come home? Above all, why did Bobe lie silent and watchful like some aged, flesh-and-blood seismograph?

Day after day, the questions had swirled in Becka's head like fish in a bowl. No answers had followed. Only more questions.

Was she herself in some way responsible for the family's unhappiness?

"Judith and Becka—it is as if the sun had brought forth the moon," she had once heard one of her mother's friends murmur. But her parents themselves had never seemed to mind that their only daughter had inherited, not her mother's golden Jewish beauty, but her father's thick black hair, his Irish-blue eyes, and his funny, crooked nose and mouth.

"Have you noticed, Patrick, that our Becka is growing prettier every day?" Judith demanded regularly.

Indeed, in particular, her mother, had always seemed delighted with Becka's love of music. And she could not think that in musical progress she was failing anyone. Miss Royal, who, as Ginny had once giggled, "gives out compliments as often as a peanut-vending machine spits bubble gum," sat through her lessons this year in unmistakable satisfaction. "Someday soon you can start on the Paganini Caprices," she promised.

Judith herself was increasingly, almost bewilderingly generous with praise. One afternoon, when Becka was practicing as usual, Judith came bursting into her room with a tape recorder.

"I'm going to tape that marvelous Chaconne. Play it all the way through again, Becka, if you don't mind," she cried.

"I don't know why. You hear it every day."

"I could never hear that Bach too often. And you play it so beautifully."

When the taping was finished, Judith applauded.

"Wonderful! Papa Bach would be happy. No one so young has a right to play so well."

"*You* were playing the harp in Junior Symphony when you were thirteen," Becka protested, but Judith gave her head a deprecatory toss.

"When I was thirteen, I was only blowing soap bubbles.

My notes were beautiful, but you could have poked your finger right through them. No mind. No heart. You have everything together already. What more can I say?"

You could tell me about the secret in this house.

But Becka did not speak the words aloud. She would not have dared, even if her mother had not turned and hurried from the room. Soon Judith was in Bobe's bedroom, demanding eagerly, "Did you hear her, Bobe, darling? We are harboring a genius."

"And is that such a surprise?" came the fierce *ha-rumph.*

No, the O'Brien problem was not Becka's music. What, then?

It had been just two days before the bewildering visit with Bobe that Becka had had her first hint of an answer. One of Pittsburgh's heavy midwinter storms had fallen upon the city, snapping power lines, clogging highways, and bringing early school dismissal. Blown along upon the snow-laden wind, Becka had waved good-bye to Ginny Witherspoon on Ellsworth Avenue and reached St. James Place at an unaccustomed two o'clock.

Shivering, she had let herself in at the side entrance so that she would not track the hall, pulled off her snow-ribboned jacket and boots, and dropped her soaking mittens down upon them. To her surprise, she heard no music from beyond the closed door of the living room—Judith's beloved sanctuary with its music stands, its shelves piled high with scores, and, of course, her harp, like a golden dragon's wing in the bright bay window.

The storm must have canceled the usual Wednesday

afternoon rehearsal, Becka decided. Instead of music, she heard two earnest voices. Judith's and Mrs. Witherspoon's. Judith and Ginny's mother had been best friends since childhood.

Mrs. Witherspoon seemed to be taking a deep, unnatural breath.

"It's fine to be broad-minded, Judith. I'd be the last to criticize. Still, I wonder whether you may not be inviting serious trouble by approving of this trip to Seven Springs," she murmured.

"I don't think so, Virginia. It's to be for only four days. Just a long skiing weekend. Patrick and Marcy have been working terribly hard on that complicated Mesta case ever since Christmas. Patrick says he could never find another secretary to keep up such a pace, and I know that's true. They both deserve a break."

There was a short silence. Then, without warning, Judith's voice changed.

"You must see how things stand, Virginia. Both Patrick and Marcy adore skiing, but I hate shivering on those icy slopes. Besides, I couldn't possibly get away from the city. I've a rash of rehearsals for my concert next month. I have to remember that, first of all, I'm a harpist. I can't risk spraining or breaking anything. Or staying out in the cold so long that I crack my fingertips. You *do* see, Virginia?"

"I see that a harp is a demanding mistress," Mrs. Witherspoon answered slowly, and all at once there were sobs. Mrs. Witherspoon's or Judith's? Becka could not be certain. She had never heard her mother cry.

The sound went with her, clear and frightening, as she climbed the hall stairs with silent, weighted steps.

On a morning soon after Patrick's return from Seven Springs, Bobe gave them all a truly frightening surprise. Becka wakened to hear the old woman's voice shrilling out an incomprehensible tangle of sound. With a swift thrust at her blankets, she jumped up and hurried across the hall. Judith and Patrick were there before her, leaning over the big brass bed, trying to soothe the tiny figure in the wildly tossing covers.

"There, there, Bobe, you must have had a nightmare, but you're all right now," Judith crooned, pressing her cheek against the wrinkled one.

"You're safe, dear," Patrick echoed. Patrick's kind, slightly lopsided face reflected Judith's concern. He had never known his own grandparents, he had once explained to Becka, and so Bobe had always been his special treasure. Her eighty-fourth birthday last autumn had seemed a kind of miracle to him. "Are you listening to me, Bobe? *You are here at home.*"

But nothing seemed to have any effect upon the old woman. She continued to thrash about, throwing her comforter awry and pausing in her outcry only long enough to take a shallow breath before she screamed again.

Becka listened in horror.

"Whatever is she saying? I can't make out a word."

"Nor can I." Patrick shook his head miserably. "She might be speaking a foreign language."

Judith looked at him indignantly. "Of course! Can't you

tell—it's Yiddish!" Then, as quickly as it had come, the color faded from her cheeks. "Sorry. How *could* you tell that, Patrick? Heaven knows, we never hear Yiddish in this house. Bobe always insisted we were an American family, though she did try to teach me a little Yiddish when I was small. She wanted to amuse me, since Mama was ill so often and I needed attention. If only I could remember—oh, if I only could!"

Then the babble began to sort itself out ever so slightly. Becka could make out letter sounds, even syllables.

"Listen, Judith. She's saying something like 'doctor.' Doctor. Don't you hear her?"

"Why, yes, you're right! Dr. Cohn. She wants Dr. Cohn. Go phone him, Patrick. I'm sure he'll come since he's just around the corner. He's watched over her for so many years."

Even as Patrick left the room to make the call, Bobe's babble grew less insistent, her tiny body tossed less violently.

"That may be what she wanted." Judith's worried frown deepened. "Oh, poor thing, whatever is wrong with her? Can she have had such a really dreadful nightmare?"

"Bobe always had *beautiful* dreams. She told me so," Becka murmured, but Judith, distraught, was no longer listening.

"Do lie still, dear. You must not wear yourself out. Dr. Cohn will be coming soon."

Indeed, when Patrick returned, it was with welcome news.

"Dr. Cohn will stop by in just a short while before he goes to make his hospital rounds."

"Oh, good, Patrick! Good! Thank heaven, he speaks Yiddish."

Now that help was so near, Judith seemed anxious for Becka to be on her way to school.

"You needn't stay here, darling. Dr. Cohn will do whatever needs to be done. If he finds anything seriously wrong, we'll telephone school at once."

Patrick darted his wife an uncertain glance, but Judith stood firm.

"It's a sunny morning. You'll have a nice walk."

In fact, the air and the chatter of the other girls who joined Becka along the way, and even Ginny Witherspoon's sympathetic hand squeeze when she whispered the news about Bobe, only made her distress spin more rapidly.

After the first class, she went to the nurse's office.

"My head. Drums are pounding in it."

"I can let you lie down for an hour, Rebecca," the nurse said. "A quiet rest may be all you need. Or, if you feel too ill, I will call your parents."

"Call my parents, please."

Patrick came for her promptly, offering apologies as she slipped into the front seat of the waiting Buick.

"I'm afraid your mother didn't realize how upset you were. She was so worried about Bobe. Your mother can get pretty preoccupied. Sorry, presh." When he was especially moved, he used the pet name, short for "precious," for both Judith and herself.

Becka managed a wan smile.

"Has Dr. Cohn come yet?"

"He'd been delayed, but he was with Bobe when I left the house."

"What do you think is wrong with her, Patrick?"

"I only wish I knew."

At home, Judith and Dr. Cohn, a big, grizzled man with the quiet confidence of many years of practice, were coming down the stairs when Becka bounded through the front door, Patrick only a few steps behind her. Judith was shaking her head bewilderedly.

"Oh, Dr. Cohn, I could never have guessed such a thing! Why should Bobe want to go to a *nursing home*? *This* is her home. She's lived here for nearly sixty years. And we all adore her. It makes no sense at all." Then, as the two reached the foot of the stairs: "The problem isn't that there is something dreadfully wrong with her—her heart or—well, something she doesn't want us to know?"

Dr. Cohn shook his head comfortingly. He had known Bobe, as he had often reminded them, when he had been a young boy and she the wife of a rising young jeweler in the Hill District. Like her, he had been born in Eastern Europe and, despite the passage of so many years, he spoke with that flavor still faintly upon his tongue.

"Not to worry. Bobe's health is very much as it has been for some time, Judith. She's in no new peril. She's not keeping any health secrets from you. I admit it's a surprise to me, too, that she is asking to be moved, but I think she has simply used this—this rather startling way to make sure she will be heard."

"Why?"

"Yes, why?" Patrick echoed, as he led them all into the

big, oak-paneled study with its tall bookshelves full of Grandpa Berkowitz's law books and his law school diploma in its gold frame above the mantelpiece.

"I'm afraid I can't say why. I do think, however, you should take Bobe's request seriously." Dr. Cohn seated himself in the leather chair beside the wide mahogany desk. "Old people have the right to have their wishes respected. You know, there's a nursing home near here on Negley Avenue. We could place her there, and you could visit her regularly. She'd be well cared for. I can vouch for that."

Perched miserably upon a footstool, Judith seemed skeptical. "Are you sure you understand what she has told you? You're certain?"

"Positive," Dr. Cohn replied firmly. "She still speaks excellent Yiddish, you know."

"And that's so ridiculous, too." Judith clenched her long, harpist's fingers. "To go back to Yiddish—to refuse to talk to us. Bobe's English has always been so good. With hardly a trace of an accent. She told me once that she began taking language lessons as soon as she got to Pittsburgh because she didn't want to be thought a dummy. . . . Not that anybody ever thought Bobe dumb. She was a clever businesswoman, as we all know. And she was such a leader of the women at temple."

Dr. Cohn nodded in agreement.

"Still, this can happen, Judith. The very old, no matter how clever, sometimes go back to the speech of their childhood. They forget the years between."

"Bobe hasn't forgotten anything." Again Judith shook her head. "Her body is feeble, but her mind is sharp. She knows everything that goes on in this house, and she knows exactly what she's doing now. I am certain of that. Only, *what* is she doing? I wish I could understand."

It was Becka who responded, hours later, when Judith was still pacing the house searching for answers.

"Maybe Bobe just doesn't like us, Judith. Maybe she doesn't like the way we act. She doesn't want to send us away, so instead she's leaving us behind."

"Oh, Becka, what a strange thing to say! How could that possibly be true? We're her family."

Bewildered as the rest of them might be, no one could doubt Bobe's determination. Every morning, Becka awoke to hear a soft babble of Yiddish and the sound of moving covers from the bedroom across the hall. It was as if Bobe were letting them know that she could break into a tantrum again at any moment if she felt her will might be ignored. All day long, she refused to speak English. Her only messages came through Dr. Cohn.

The family had no choice but to do as she demanded. Patrick made the arrangements.

On a blustery Saturday morning in March, he carried Bobe, along with her great down comforter and cocoon of pillows and sheets, downstairs and out to a waiting ambulance. For her going-away gift, he had presented her with a new tape recorder and earphones so that she could listen to her music whenever she wished. Judith had given her a half-dozen new nightgowns in lovely pastel shades, all trimmed with dollops of lace. The gowns were folded into a shiny red box which Bobe clutched beneath the comforter.

"The nursing home will never have had such a sexy guest," Patrick teased, but Bobe only continued to stare straight ahead. She seemed as determined not to understand them as to ensure that they should not understand her.

Following the small procession to the curb, Becka watched as Patrick and the ambulance attendant settled their slight burden onto a stretcher. It was then that Judith came rushing from the house, frantically thrusting her arms into the sleeves of a bulky Aran sweater.

"I will ride with her. You must let me," she cried.

The attendant nodded permission. Still Bobe showed no sign that she noticed Judith or any of them. Only at the very last moment, when the ambulance door was closing, did the tiny head half-lift from the puff of pillow.

"Bobe!" Becka gasped, and she saw the little hand with the misshapen finger stir ever so slightly beneath the covers, saw the curve of the pale, dry lips.

"A gutn tag, maidele." A tear glittered on the wrinkled cheeks.

" *'A gutn tag, maidele.'* It means 'Good-bye, girl,' " Judith explained when she returned from the nursing home. "Bobe was crying when she said that. She didn't really want to go away. Why, oh, why has she done this?"

Later, as days passed and Bobe refused to see either Becka or Patrick, Judith grew angry. Becka knew that was her mother's way when she was deeply frightened or upset.

"Bobe is a witch! Oh, truly she is a witch of an old

woman!" Judith exclaimed one night at dinner after a long and fruitless visit. "I sat beside her bed for two hours, and she wouldn't say a word in English. I know she understood what the nurses were saying, because she did exactly what they asked. Took her medicine. Let them turn her in the bed. Nodded when they checked off her menu. Oh, I could have shaken her."

"Why don't the three of us take in a movie tonight, presh? We might all feel better," Patrick suggested shyly.

But in her hurt and fury, Judith had overturned her water goblet and did not hear him.

"Good heavens, I'd forgotten!" she cried as she leaped up from the table to escape the spreading pool. "Myra Hottel is coming tonight so that we can practice Byron McCullogh's beastly new duet. Why does that man insist on writing such difficult music?"

As the weeks went by and she was immersed in rehearsals, Judith grew calmer and more accepting of Bobe's choice. Patrick grew quieter and put in even longer hours at work. It was Becka who was left with the emptiness in the house, an emptiness which only her music could at least partially fill.

One day she took her violin into Bobe's bedroom, set up her music stand beside the bay window, and did her practicing there. If she did not look directly at the big brass bed, she could almost imagine that Bobe still lay there, that she was playing to her, that the white head was once again stirring with approval—and, above all, that Bobe's silence and rejection had ended.

It was there in Bobe's bedroom that Judith found Becka

one bright April afternoon. For the first time in many weeks, Judith looked, not calm or accepting or preoccupied, but jubilant. As she came through the doorway, she joyously held out a letter.

"Stop playing this minute, Becka. News! Wonderful news! Read this!"

The words on the official-looking sheet of paper swam before Becka's eyes.

Dear Rebecca, This is to inform you . . . a scholarship . . . our new summer program at Tanglewood . . . we should feel honored. . . .

"But I don't understand, Judith."

"No, of course, you don't. How could you?" Judith recaptured the paper and waved it triumphantly before her. "To go back to the beginning. You remember all those weeks ago when I taped the Chaconne? That wasn't just my little game, you know. I sent that tape to Tanglewood, along with a detailed statement of your training and Miss Royal's recommendation. I'd just read that they're starting a new program for very young musicians. For years they've brought promising students to the summer festival to hear the symphony and have a chance to play with topnotch professionals. They've never before invited people your age.

"It's to be a very small experimental group for this first year. The announcement said they would take only twenty young teenagers from around the country, but you are developing so beautifully that Miss Royal thought you would have a chance. I thought so, too. And Bobe was certain of it.

"We were right. You've been accepted. Isn't it wonderful?"

Becka felt Judith's arm go around her, felt Judith's breath upon her cheek, felt mingled doubt and delight.

"Tanglewood? I've never been there. Is it far?"

"Not really. Just in western Massachusetts. Patrick or I could drive you up there in a day."

"I'd have to stay alone?"

"Well, yes. That is, you'd be with your group, of course. You wouldn't want a parent hanging around as if you were some little kid."

"How long would I stay?"

"Eight weeks. From the middle of June to the middle of August. The dates are there in the letter. Oh, it will be such a marvelous chance for you. Maybe even the beginning of a professional career. Chatham Music Day Camp is wonderful, and you've had lovely times there. But playing another summer with all those kids, sweet as they are—you'd be bored to extinction. Time to move on."

Slowly Becka took herself from her mother's arms. The familiar room with the bay window, the bed, the poster on the wall, even her violin and music stand seemed to tremble before her in an unsteady wash of color. The floor dipped.

Twenty teenagers from around the country? Was it true that she played so well? Excitement hammered at her pulse . . . and yet . . . and yet . . .

"Does—does Patrick know all this? Does he want me to go?"

Judith drew back, the lines of her face hardening, the happiness fading.

"Yes, to both questions," she said, nodding tensely. "Though we didn't plan it this way originally—you must believe that we didn't—still, this makes other things possible."

"Other things?"

"Yes. You see, Becka, this summer isn't going to be a—a different time just for you. It's going to be different for all three of us. I've been asked to tour Europe and play in a marvelous series of concerts. I never thought I would have such a chance."

"You're leaving Patrick alone?"

"N-no. That is, not exactly." Judith flushed scarlet. "Patrick—Patrick wants to try a new kind of life, too. On a strictly trial basis, of course. An experiment. You've got to know the truth sometime, Becka. It might as well be now. Patrick wants to spend the summer with—with—"

"With *Marcy*?"

"I thought you might have guessed." Judith nodded, drawing in a long breath. She looked over Becka's head, out the window at the sky or the house across the street or maybe not at anything at all. Her voice was far away.

"This all began such a long time ago. Your father was the brightest young member of Grandpa Berkowitz's firm, you know. Just out of University of Pennsylvania Law School. A prodigy. He could never have guessed that the night your grandpa brought him home to dinner, he'd find a girl playing a harp and fall head over heels in love with her—that we would both fall in love. We were a kind of revelation to each other.

"I had never known anyone who had put himself through college and law school, earning every penny he had ever spent. Patrick had never before met a Jewish 'princess' who'd never so much as boiled an egg or washed her own stockings—who was a dedicated musician. Our marriage was bound to be hard."

"But you say you fell in love with him," Becka protested. "I'd have thought you'd want to make him happy."

Judith's lips went white.

"I did fall in love with him. I—I love him still. And I wanted to make him happy. I just don't seem to have succeeded. Patrick tells me he feels, well, comfortable with Marcy. She's Irish Catholic, like him in a lot of ways. When he first met me, he must have thought that those background things don't matter. In the long run, maybe he's finding that they do."

"You—you are really telling me, then—" Becka fought against the tears that threatened to block her words—"you're saying that—that this summer is just an excuse. You and Patrick are separating. You're letting someone else have him. We're not going to be a family anymore."

"I'm not telling you anything of the kind!" Judith flung about, her face flaming, angry, desperate. "Oh, I did think you would be mature about this, Becka. I thought I could trust you to understand. I've told you this is an experiment. For all of us. A chance for Patrick to find out whether—whether someone else means more to him than I do. A chance for me to find out whether music means more to me than Patrick does. Above all, a chance for you to develop as a violinist. A chance for you to grow at Tanglewood."

"But I'm not going to Tanglewood." Becka shook her head, swiftly, fiercely deciding. "I'm not going to go away. I'm going to keep us all together in this house."

She had never had such a fight with her mother. They screamed at each other as Becka had never imagined they could do.

"I thought, of course, that you could see all this coming, Becka. Or did you refuse to see? And you don't seem to realize that you're being offered a very great honor at Tanglewood. There must be hundreds of kids all over the country who'd give their eyeteeth for the chance you're spitting on.

"Anyhow, you can't possibly believe we would let you stay in this house alone all summer. Or that, at this late date, Patrick and I can change our plans."

"I would have Mrs. Capek."

"Mrs. Capek is not here evenings and weekends. She has her own family, that sick daughter and all those poor runny-nosed little grandchildren. She'd never abandon them. You know that as well as I do."

"Nothing would happen to me here."

"That's just the point. Part of it, at least. Musically, absolutely nothing would happen to you here. Whereas, in Tanglewood—"

"But I'm not going to Tanglewood."

"Oh, must we go round and round in the same circle? I did think you were cleverer, Becka. I am so disappointed in you. I thought that you would see."

Becka shook her head despairingly.

"One thing I *do* see. You were never a good wife to

Patrick. You never even gave up your name. It's always Judith Berkowitz, not just on your concert programs but wherever you go with him. I can tell he doesn't really like that. And now you're trying to give him away. As if he were an old coat that might fit somebody else better. You'll be lucky if he ever speaks to you again."

And then, at last, Judith turned frighteningly, icily cold.

"I don't like to pull rank on you, Becka. With first names and all the rest, Patrick and I have always tried not to do that. But you are making it necessary now. No matter how you feel, you are to spend this coming weekend with the Witherspoons. Absolutely no protest allowed. Your father and I must have time to get away somewhere—to neutral ground—and talk out this absurd situation."

"I'll ask Patrick—"

"No use. You won't get a chance to wangle a reprieve from him. He phoned to say he's working late on a big case. *As usual,* I might point out. Or hadn't you noticed?"

At least, for one more time, the two of them would be going away together, not with someone else, Becka told herself as she crept toward her own room and threw herself upon the bed. Shrunken didn't describe how she felt. Rather, it was as if the emptiness that had opened up inside her with Bobe's departure now threatened to expand to include her whole body. How could emptiness be so heavy? How could it hurt so much?

Judith apologized the next day.

"I don't know how I could have said such things to you, darling. It was my dreadful temper. I must try to improve. It was just that I was startled by your reaction. You were startled, too, I suppose. Forgive, sweet?"

Apology, however, did not lighten Becka's sadness. Her body tense and hard, she fought her way out of the arms that Judith tried to throw about her.

"I'm still going to the Witherspoons this weekend?" she demanded in a thin, small voice.

"Why, yes. Yes, of course. You're to go there directly after school on Friday. Virginia agreed at once. She said I should tell you that you're always welcome in that house."

And that was to be Ginny Witherspoon's solution to the whole dreadful problem.

"Mom says you can stay here in our house all summer! Oh, won't it be wonderful, Becka?"

Not that Ginny had a chance to make her proposal until very late that Saturday evening. Becka had resolved that she would not talk about what was happening in her family, no matter how much Judith might have confessed to Mrs. Witherspoon. She *could* not tell. It would be like saying, "You don't recognize it, Gin, but I'm not your best friend anymore. I'm not a real person. I'm not even here. First it was Bobe who went away. Next Judith and Patrick. Now me."

Ginny wouldn't understand that. Everything always looked bright to her. She wasn't even concerned that her braces made her look as if somebody had pasted a row of huge, silvery fish scales across her teeth. Or that she was the tallest eighth grader at Winchester. Or that she was so clumsy that every afternoon she tripped over the rug in her front hall when she came home from school.

"Mom says I'm growing so fast my parts don't fit to-gether right," Ginny often apologized, laughing. "She says that basically I've got good bone structure. One day I'll be gorgeous. I just have to wait."

With all her awkwardness, Ginny had a disposition as sunny as her flyaway yellow hair.

"They're good for each other, those two girls," their mothers had long since agreed. "Becka keeps Ginny from being self-satisfied. Ginny keeps Becka sensible and relaxed. A balance wheel."

All that bright, cool Saturday, however, as the two played violin and viola duets, wandered the few blocks to Shadyside Village to window-shop and browse in Pinocchio's Book Store, and later as they ate pizza in the Witherspoon's familiar family room, the balance wheel did not work. Becka was engulfed in her silent misery, and Ginny was unnaturally fluttery and restless, alternately twisting the TV dial and flop-ping down on the shag rug to practice gymnastics even more clumsily than usual.

At eleven o'clock, Mrs. Witherspoon called down the stairs that they were to come to bed. A few minutes later, as they pulled up the smooth, cool covers and settled down beside each other in the darkness, Becka could no longer keep silent. In spite of her earlier resolve, she burst out with the story of the Tanglewood scholarship.

"Is *that* what you've been mooning about all day? No wonder you seemed miles away!" Ginny bounced upon the bed as though she were a pillow that someone had abruptly plumped. "Why, it's fantastic, Becka! Of course, I'm not surprised. You deserve it. You've always played better than any of the rest of us. Miss Royal says you're her most gifted pupil."

"But I'm not going to go to Tanglewood."

"Oh!" The sound was like a suddenly bursting balloon. Then, turning on her side, Ginny excitedly made the suggestion.

"If you don't want to go away, you can stay here with us all summer. I'm positive Mom will say yes. You can live here, and we can go to music camp together just as we've done for years. I mean, Chatham would be boring without you. Just me and all those goopy kids."

"They're not goopy kids. Besides, you don't understand, Ginny. I don't want to stay here. I am going to stay in my own house." Becka clenched her fists beneath the covers. For a moment, Ginny lay still.

"Oh!" she said again. "Well, after all, why not?"

"The problem is, Gin, that Judith and Patrick—well, they're going away for a while, and they won't let me stay home alone."

"Mrs. Capek could stay with you, couldn't she?"

"Judith won't hear of that."

"You don't think it's because Mrs. Capek is a love child?"

Ginny continued to be entranced by the fact that good, cheery Mrs. Capek, who had the build of a Steeler linebacker and hands like Brillo pads, always wore a pair of delicate diamond earrings. She had told the girls the story of the earrings one day when they had at last gathered courage to ask.

Years ago, Mrs. Capek's mother had hired out as a maid

in a rich household in Prague, Bohemia, and had fallen in love with the son of the family. The young man had loved her, too, but his parents had refused to let him marry a poor country girl, and so he had given her the earrings and sent her away to America to marry a carpenter who had immigrated there from her village. Not long after that, Mrs. Capek had been born.

Becka shook her head in the darkness.

"I don't think Judith worries about things like that, Gin. She just says Mrs. Capek can't leave her family, and I guess that's true. But I've got to stay at home. I've got to. I couldn't bear to go so far away when—when—well, you see, it's all a dreadful problem."

"I see. Y-yes. That is, I guess . . ." This time, Ginny's unaccustomed silence ended, not with a fresh flow of words, but with a yawn.

"Sorry, Becka. I can't seem to hold my eyes open any longer. I'll think about all this tomorrow morning. There must be some—some way . . ." And she curled into a warm knot and fell asleep immediately.

Becka could not close her eyes. The minutes passed slowly as she lay staring into the dark room, seeing the fuzzy outline of Ginny's furniture, hearing the foreign house sounds.

Those sounds made her tremble. She had often stayed overnight with Ginny, but by midnight she had always been too happily exhausted to do anything but fall asleep. She had never listened before.

The night sounds at home were comfortingly familiar. The click of the furnace as it snapped on or off. The faraway rumble of the refrigerator. The creak of old boards. The sigh of a breeze at an open window.

Whereas, here—she jounced suddenly upright. The grandfather's clock in the hall downstairs was bonging! One-two-three-four-five-six-seven-eight-nine-ten-eleven-twelve. How could anyone stay asleep? Later, she heard the one o'clock bong, solemn and lingering. Had she truly stayed awake so long?

She felt herself falling back and forth between sleeping and waking, as if across the threshold of some dark doorway, without the strength or will to decide on which side she should linger. And then she was in the midst of horror! She was standing in front of her own home in daylight so bright that even the tiniest details were clear enough to sting her eyes— the front door, with its glittering stained-glass fanlight, the bay window beyond which stood Judith's harp, as visible as though the stout brick walls had become transparent, the upstairs bay window, and beyond it, Bobe's shining bed. Suddenly everything about the house glinted, brilliant as a fireball.

Becka threw up her hands to shield her eyes. When she dropped them again, *the house had vanished*! Fallen into a giant hole which, like the inverted scoop of some greedy earthmover, was gradually eating away the whole of St. James Place. One by one, houses slid over the lip of that monstrous excavation and fell out of sight.

Before all of them could disappear, she had reached for her shoes, pulled her brown parka on over her pajamas, and made her way, fingers desperately groping, past the furniture in Ginny's darkened bedroom. A night light shone dimly in the hall below, just illuminating the face of the grandfather's clock and its gilded, curlicue-tipped fingers. One twenty-five.

When she reached the bottom of the stairs, the latch on the Witherspoons' front door proved to be double-tripped. It took time to open. She managed to turn the knob at last and let herself out onto the porch.

The cool night air washed across her heated cheeks. An uneasy chill shot through her, as she moved resolutely on down the porch steps. She had never walked alone so late at night—Patrick and Judith would not have allowed it, even if she had asked permission—yet home was only four blocks away, and she knew the neighborhood well. Although her uneasiness increased with each passing minute, she was certain that she would not get lost, would reach St. James Place quickly.

Along the sidewalks, the spoon-shaped streetlamps made dim pools of light, and she hurried through the shadows laced between those pale beacons. As she rounded the corner of her street, she gave an astonished gasp. The house was still there! Gratefully she rushed up the steps, across the old-fashioned porch, toward the front door, where the stained-glass fanlight shone in bright green leaves and tendrils, rose and yellow flowers.

Judith must have forgotten to turn off the light in the hall before her departure. That was her usual way. She also must have, as usual, forgotten to lock the front door, since the knob twisted easily. At least Becka would not have to grope for the key hidden in the false lintel brick. Breath tightening, she slipped past the door into the hall.

The light high in the ceiling did not penetrate the shadows on the stairs before her. The house itself seemed mysterious and unwelcoming. For a heart-pounding moment, she nearly turned back toward the Witherspoons'. But that would be to reenter a dark night without the force of her dream to give her courage.

She dared not pause to flip a light switch. Instead, she hurried on up the sweeping stairs, bent upon reaching the safety of her own room. It was only at the head of those stairs that she stopped dead still. To her right, the door of her parents' room stood open, and she could see in the dim glow of the night light that a great pile of Patrick's and Judith's clothing had been thrown across the bed. One of Judith's suitcases stood open and upended beside the closet door.

Yet more surprising, at the far end of the hall, beyond Becka's own room, a just perceptible wing of light lay motionless upon the polished floor. The attic door was open!

"Stuff! Sixty years of stuff stored away in that attic!" Judith had once exclaimed to Mrs. Capek. "I must get Bobe to let us sort out things up there." But Mrs. Capek had frowned her habitual disapproval of even the most gentle attack upon Bobe's ways, and Judith had backed off. "One day we must do the job. I wonder what we will discover."

The scurry of mice was what Becka and Ginny had found one afternoon last autumn after Bobe, stern mistress of the mysteries above, had taken to her bed and they had gone up to explore. Confronted by the mice, or perhaps it had been by their own consciences, they had scuttled guiltily back down the steep steps before they could have any clear view of the wide, shadowy space above. Ginny had stumbled, as usual, before she reached the last narrow tread, and had fallen the rest of the way down on her knees.

"Don't scrub up the blood, Becka," she had laughed through her pain. "It looks so—so gross. You know, like the blood spot they say never fades away in the palace of Mary, Queen of Scots." Ginny was a great lover of historical mysteries and murders.

Practical Mrs. Capek had long since washed away Ginny's blood, and no one else had known about the girls' abortive adventure.

But who could be in the attic now at two o'clock in the morning?

Not Patrick, surely. With his careful ways, her father would never have left the front door unlocked or his clothes tossed upon the bed. Her mother? Yes, it could well be that Judith had not gone away after all. Perhaps at the last moment Patrick had been too busy to make the trip. Perhaps they had quarreled. Had Judith, then, left alone in the house at midnight, too upset to sleep or practice, impulsively gone up to straighten the long-neglected attic?

Becka moved cautiously along the hall. "Judith . . . Judith." There was a movement above, but no voice answered her. Panting softly, hands propping her between the enclosing walls, Becka started up the narrow stairs.

In the big room above, a small unshaded lightbulb, hung from a dangling cord, shone faintly, casting alternate patches of light and shadow. No one could have seen that light from outside, for only a narrow dormer window, shade drawn tightly shut, faced St. James Place. The surprise was that she could not see her mother. Tall old boxes and battered trunks, a clutter of dusty furniture, piles of books and records, an old-fashioned china washbowl and pitcher, a chest of discarded drapes—all stood in lonely silence. The nearest boxes had been overturned. Their spilled contents lay in a jumble upon the floor.

Her mother must be somewhere, hidden in the shadows, not speaking for her own reasons. Perhaps suspecting a stranger?

A stranger! All at once, Becka's pulse tripped wildly. What if she had made a mistake? "Judith! Judith, it's me. B-Becka." She struggled to call one more time and then stopped, unable to go on.

On the floor at her feet, beside an upturned corrugated cardboard carton, lay a pile of yellowed papers and pictures and, uppermost, the photograph of a young girl. Trembling, she stooped and picked it up.

Mounted on thick photographic cardboard, the picture was browned at the edges, but it had at some time been tinted in pastel colors so that it glowed with a kind of inner light. The girl, ten or eleven years old, stood in a stiff, old-fashioned pose. She wore a blue tam and a matching jumper that fell below her knees. A thick braid of red hair hung over one shoulder, and her eyes were blue-green and remarkably sharp.

The face in the photograph was strange, yet at the same time mysteriously familiar. Fingers damp with nervousness, Becka turned the picture over. A name was written across the back in faded brown ink, in a curlicue script. Hannah Eliashov. Hannah Eliashov? She stooped again.

On the floor were other pictures that had tumbled out of a large envelope. Two little boys in short smocks and long stockings. A young woman with waist squeezed tight, her earnest face surmounted by dark, tightly drawn hair. A burly young man who looked as though his enormous shoulders would burst through the sleeves of the coat the photographer must have insisted that he wear. Names were written on the backs of these pictures, also. Uri, Leibel, Rachel, Moishe.

The pictures slipped from Becka's hands. Only the girl with the thick red braid and the piercing eyes continued to stare up at her.

Hannah. Hannah Eliashov.

It was as she still stooped, repeating the name to herself, that she saw another bag not nearly so dusty or so old. Plastic. From Radio Shack. This bag, too, had been upended and its contents spilled out upon the floor. But these were not pictures. These were tape cassettes, neatly numbered and labeled.

That labeling, Becka saw with a gasp, had been done in Grandpa Berkowitz's careful hand, a hand which she knew well from the letters and gifts that came regularly from Florida. The labeling read Bobe's Story.

Bobe's Story. Bobe. Hannah. Hannah Eliashov. Of course! Eliashov was the name on the Carnegie Hall poster, and when Dr. Cohn spoke directly to Bobe, he called her Hannah. . . .

But Becka had no more time to think. As she rose to her feet, dropping the tapes into her deep parka pockets for safekeeping, she saw that she indeed had a companion in the attic room, and that companion was not Judith. It was a man in a ski mask, who emerged from the shadows in the far corner and advanced swiftly toward her. He was holding an open violin case in which a dusty instrument lay against cobwebby green velvet.

All at once he set the violin down and seized up a length of dark drapery from the chest beside him. In a swift lasso, he threw the curtain forward so that its stifling folds settled over Becka's head.

With a cry she struggled to break free, but the curtain blinded and hobbled her. The man was winding it tight about her body. Again she struggled, the cloth coarse against her cheeks, her lips, her tongue. With a desperate surge of strength she managed to throw herself backward toward the stairs. And then she was falling . . . falling into searing pain. Into blackness.

The catapult was the strongest force that Becka had ever known. It was thrusting her swiftly forward. She was a circus performer shot from a giant cannon. She was crashing through a high hoop, ripping the paper that covered it into streaming ribbons of color.

From beyond the hoop, a voice spoke.

"You've had a bad bump on the head, Becka, dear, but you mustn't be frightened. Dr. Cohn thinks you're going to be quite all right."

Vaguely, sensing herself to be in her own bed and yet at

the same time floating somewhere very far away, she struggled to hold her eyes open and look about her.

The voice was Mrs. Witherspoon's. It was Mrs. Witherspoon who bent above her. At a greater distance were other figures, more like mirror reflections than solid flesh. Dr. Cohn, Mr. Witherspoon, Ginny.

"Sorry to rat on you, but I had to tell Mom when I woke up and found you were gone," Ginny whispered.

"*Luckily* she told us!" Mrs. Witherspoon leaned yet closer, her face blotting out other sights and sounds. "Your parents were down at Oglebay Park. We have telephoned them. They should be here soon."

But already Becka was drifting, only by desperate effort keeping her hold upon her last discovery before the masked figure had risen from the attic shadows.

"The tapes!" she whispered. "Bobe's story. I want—I want—"

And, after all, she could not hold on but was lost once more in darkness.

Hours passed. Many hours. Or at least she supposed so, since, when she reawakened, her bedroom was sunlit and two quite solid faces had replaced the ghostly four that had surrounded her as she came crashing through the circus hoop. Judith and Patrick.

"Oh, Patrick, look, she's stirring! Becka, do open your eyes!"

"Speak to us, presh."

She felt herself smiling at them weakly, yet not wanting to talk at all.

"Bobe's story," she managed. "I want to hear Bobe's story."

"What on earth is Bobe's story?"

"What do you mean, presh?"

"I mean the tapes. They're in my parka pockets. I—I found them just before I saw the man."

"The man? You *saw* a man, darling?"

"Only just. He was wearing a ski mask."

"Thank God he doesn't seem to have laid a hand on you." Patrick's lips trembled. "He does seem to have made a bit of a mess pawing through the bedrooms. Through the attic, too. I gather he must have fled when you fell down the attic stairs, probably afraid that he'd be held responsible for any injury to you."

"He was a beast! Not to find out whether you *had* been hurt," Judith declared, dashing a hand across her eyes.

Becka felt herself drifting.

"I want to hear the tapes," she repeated dreamily.

"What tapes? She can't know what she's saying, Patrick."

But Patrick had moved to the chair on which someone had laid Becka's parka, and he was digging deep into the bulging pockets.

"She's right, Judith," he exclaimed. "There are tapes here. A half-dozen of them. They're—why, they're marked Bobe's Story, and in your father's handwriting. I remember, now, his telling us that he had once persuaded Bobe to talk about herself. Probably she regretted it afterward and squirreled the tapes away. That would be like her. She's always been so private. . . . But, you see—" Patrick's voice dropped to a whisper—"Becka's mind is clear."

"Thank heaven for that." Judith's voice also grew softer. "Still, I don't think she should be fretting over such things. Dr. Cohn said that although her vital signs are perfect, she must lie absolutely quiet until he's sure she can be safely taken to the hospital for X-rays."

"I am aware of all that, presh," Patrick said, nodding patiently, "but she'll fret doubly if we don't let her listen. See how she's watching us, how her eyes plead."

Judith sighed weakly.

"You're right. She probably won't listen long, anyhow. She'll drift right back to sleep."

Becka did not drift. She did not move into the silent dark. She had known that she would not. Patrick brought the recorder to her bedside, and the tape began to unreel. At its sound, she felt gloriously bright and awake, borne along upon a swift river of voices. It was Grandpa Berkowitz's voice that came first.

"Lives like yours should be remembered, Bobe. Rebecca said that you told her very little about your childhood when she was small. With Rebecca herself so long gone and the rest of your people gone, too, or scattered, we know next to nothing. We should know, for Becka's sake when she is older. Your life—your family's life—could be important to her. Tell me your story, Bobe."

"For Becka, then, and for my family. I was always so proud of them, but I thought no one else would care." That was Bobe's voice right enough, though stronger, younger than it had been these last years. "What do you want to know? Where shall I start, David?"

"Why, at the beginning, I should think. In Poland. In the *shtetl,* your native village. What is your first memory there?"

"Music, of course."

"Music?"

"A violin. I was so tiny, Mama would scarcely let me out of her arms, but I thought that instrument made the most beautiful sound anyone could hope to hear in this life."

"Whose violin was it, Bobe? Uncle Aaron's?"

"No, no. That was long before Aaron lifted a bow. It was the fiddler's music. At Aunt Yehudis's wedding.

"Not everybody was happy about Aunt Yehudis's wedding, you know. They said she was throwing herself away on a poor cripple like Uncle Nahum. But the fiddler made them forget all that. He and his music made them dance."

"That's a beautiful beginning, Bobe. Tell me more."

"About what?" For an instant Bobe was stubborn. Not even a wily lawyer like Grandpa Berkowitz would be able to persuade her against her will. "Tell more about what, David?"

"Why, about them all. Your mama and papa. Aunt Yehudis. Aaron. Yourself. About the whole family there in the *shtetl.*"

Finally Bobe could no longer resist the gathering force of her awakened memories. Her surrender produced a river of sound that swept Becka back and back, so far it was as though she herself did not exist at all.

"My family in the *shtetl*? How could I forget them? Mama always said there was no family anywhere in the Tsar's wide realm like the Eliashovs. I thought we were the happiest family in the world. . . ."

Part Two

Hannah ✑

Of the six Eliashov children, each was truly one of a kind.

There was Rachel, the eldest, the practical one whom Mama sent to market each week to bargain with the peasant farmers for the Sabbath chicken and fish. There was Aaron, grave-eyed and handsome, with the manners of a prince. There were the twins, Chaim, round and merry, and Leibel, serious and thin. "My owl and my stork," Mama called them. There was also Muni, the wild one, and, last of all, Hannah herself, ten years younger than Rachel. In the tall, dark-haired family, she was a tiny one with flaming red curls.

Hannah was independent and strong-willed. She dreamed dreams and was curious, always eager to learn something new.

"The littlest one was not born at the beginning of this new century for nothing. She is the cleverest of all your children, Rifka," she heard Aunt Yehudis murmur one morning to Mama as the two women sat plucking goose feathers in the Eliashovs' snug whitewashed kitchen. "She sees things, that little one, though she's not yet seven years old. She thinks about what she sees. She could find her way to China and notice every stone on the path."

As Hannah stood silent in the doorway, Mama protested.

There was the ring of indignation in her voice. "How can you praise my daughter above my four fine sons?" she demanded.

But Aunt Yehudis spoke fiercely.

"I am certain that the child is clever, Rifka. You ask me how I know? What a question! Does a cucumber have to be old before you can tell it will make good food? In this I mean no affront to your Aaron, your Chaim, Leibel and Muni, or your Rachel. You should be proud of them all."

Though they had such a wealth of children, in other ways the Eliashovs were both rich and poor. Here in their higgledy-piggledy *shtetl,* like an island in the great sweep of Polish farmlands and forests, they had their own tiny home with its three, crowded rooms—the kitchen, the bedroom, and the sleeping loft for the boys. In one corner of the kitchen was the loom with which Papa earned their uncertain livelihood, and in the opposite corner, like a clumsy guardian angel, stood the brick stove that cooked their meals and kept them warm.

Outside the kitchen door, they had a kerchief of a garden figured with radishes and onions and garlic, which Mama planted in the springtime, and sometimes beets, which poked up dark blue stems to show where they were hidden in the earth.

Most important of all—though this added not a *zloty* to the family purse—they had their musical talent and the joy that came with that gift.

"If you are hungry, sing!" was Mama's motto, though spoken with a tender, sidelong glance at Papa, who, alone among them, was tone-deaf. Mama herself sang hour after hour at her work; Rachel, also. Hannah eagerly accompanied

her sister, now and again bringing her back on pitch when such
help was needed. The boys added their lusty chorus when they
were in the mood.

Only Aaron ever objected to these family concerts.

"The notes are not true today, Mama," he often protested. "Won't you tell them all to stop? They hurt my ears."

"Ho! Your poor ears!" Rachel would retort merrily,
running up the scale, flatting. "Could *you* hit such high notes
while you peeled beets, brother? Come, take my knife. I'll let
you try."

But Mama, with a shake of her beautiful head, always
defended Aaron. "Go upstairs, my son," she would murmur.
One day, when he had climbed the steps to the loft with his
head held high, she added, "He cannot help feeling pain, our
Aaron. He has perfect pitch. Such a talent. We must keep our
voices low, not disturb him. In the meantime, he does not
know I have plans."

That last mysterious statement was explained on the following unforgettable afternoon. Then Mama ceased her scrubbing and singing, as if she had been waiting for the moment,
wiped her hands upon her dark skirt, and went into the bedroom to get her velvet jewel box down from a shelf. There,
Hannah knew, Mama kept the last treasures she had from the
life of her girlhood as a rich innkeeper's daughter, a vivid
memory still of polished furniture and shining silver, of beautiful clothes and, best of all, music lessons.

That good life had been cruelly swept away by the Tsar's
soldiers and by a *pogrom,* one of those terrible raids during
which Jewish people were destroyed and their property seized.

Jews had no right to own land and fine houses, the marauders had said. Mama could never bring herself to speak of the *pogrom,* only of the shimmering days of her youth.

Now from the old treasure box she plucked a gold ring. She slipped it upon her little finger with difficulty, for the knuckles of her hands had grown knobby with the work of many years.

"I am going out," she announced to her daughters.

"I will come with you," Hannah cried, and then, as Mama shook her head, asked, "What do you mean to do?"

"You will see later. For now you must stay here with your sister like a good child."

Mama returned as the boys were coming home from school, Chaim and Muni prancing and jabbing at each other, Leibel following more cautiously, and Aaron moving with dignity behind. Hannah noticed at once. Mama no longer wore the gold ring. Instead, she carried a violin case.

At the table, she opened the case and reverently wiped her skirt across the gleaming instrument within. Hannah watched, holding her breath. For a golden instant, she seemed to hear once again the fiddle music at Aunt Yehudis's wedding, and to feel the wonder.

Then Mama proudly lifted the violin from its velvet cushions and carried it across the room. "This is for you, Aaron, my eldest," she said gravely. "Guard it well. Remember, no one else is to touch it. It is yours only to make music with, for we cannot afford a carelessly broken string."

Dark eyes shining, Aaron made a courtly bow to his mother and took the instrument into his arms. At first he cradled it awkwardly, and more than once Hannah cried out,

"No, Aaron! No! Not that way! Remember the fiddler!" But he did not need her reproof. Day after day, for hours on end, Aaron practiced the scales and exercises in Mama's tattered music books. Then, with Mama's careful instruction, he began to make music, ever and ever more beautifully.

Even Muni, the wild one, brought his friends home from school to hear Aaron play. The boys were, so Muni boasted to his sisters, the terror of the *melamed,* a scrawny young schoolteacher who hadn't the courage to complain to the boys' parents. Because of his timidity, the boys teased him unmercifully and bleated like kid goats when, in despair, he pounded his fists on his temples or pulled out strands of his pale scraggly beard or his earlocks.

Although the poor *melamed* could not keep his pupils quiet, Muni could. One threatening scowl from him and the boys, even seated in a circle on the Eliashovs' kitchen floor, became silent as bedbugs. They had no wish to feel Muni's fist in the street.

But it was clear that the boys also loved Aaron's music. They nodded and beat vigorous time to the marches. They swayed, prayerlike, to the sweet songs. When Muni nodded permission, they stomped to the dances.

One day they shook their shoulders and stomped so loudly that Mama left her mending to join them.

"It is a mazurka! Hear how Aaron plays it," she cried, and then, flushing with yet greater excitement, added, "Oh, listen! It is a Chopin mazurka! Aaron has arranged it for the violin. Who else would have dared this? Or made it turn out so well?"

Aaron himself bowed to the applause in the kitchen as

though he faced some vast audience. Hannah, seeing his delight, felt her heart swell with pride, yet she also felt a longing that choked the breath in her throat.

When would she have a chance to play?

A chance of a quite different kind came on a snowy Friday afternoon soon after her seventh birthday. The boys were already home from school. Aaron was in the loft practicing, and Chaim and Muni were wrestling in the kitchen while Leibel kept anxious watch so they would not tumble against the hot stove or out into the icy street. Stepping patiently over and around the wrestlers, Mama and Rachel were completing preparations for the Sabbath supper. Two loaves of *hallah,* the fresh white bread, were already hidden beneath a clean linen napkin on the table before Papa's place.

All at once the familiar scene was interrupted. Aunt Yehudis came bursting in at the door, little swirls of snowflakes flying about her swaying skirt and the flapping corners of her babushka. Not for independent Aunt Yehudis a wig like the one which Mama, a pious woman, wore whenever she went into the street! She did not stop to notice that she was making tracks on Mama's freshly scrubbed floor, nor did she take time for a proper greeting. Indeed, her tall, sturdy frame moved so vigorously that even Chaim and Muni became still. They stood, for once, open-mouthed.

"Great news, Rifka!" Aunt Yehudis cried. "My friend, the schoolmaster Reb Doddl, has agreed to accept Hannah as a pupil." Then, sweeping the boys out of her path with a flourish of her heavy black skirt, she rushed across the kitchen to Hannah. "You cannot know how long I have thought of this, *maidele*. I have always told your mother that you were a clever one. Now you are to prove me right. Aaron has his violin. God be praised for that. But you are to go to school!"

Hannah stood speechless. Leibel, Chaim, and Muni blinked in stunned silence. Even Chaim did not laugh. Only Mama, catching her breath, asked many questions.

"Why has Reb Doddl, such a learned man, agreed to teach a *girl*?" she demanded.

"Because I have told him he must do so! He already has two girls in his class, and he says they are as quick as the boys and more patient. They do not start fistfights when he leaves them to go out to his prayers." Aunt Yehudis darted a quick, accusing glance at Chaim and Muni, who blushed crimson, although Reb Doddl was not their master. "I have told him," she said, nodding fiercely, "that our Hannah will be a match for the best of his pupils."

"But how do you know? This is no longer a question of cucumbers. Or of stones on the road to China, Yehudis. We all love Hannah dearly, God be praised for her, yet how do you know that she can learn Hebrew, the Sacred Tongue?"

"That is easily answered. The little one spoke Yiddish before she could walk. She speaks Polish just from going with Rachel to the marketplace, from hearing her sister bargain for chicken and fresh fish."

"And from playing with the farmers' children behind the market carts while Rachel flirts with Moishe the Drayman," said Chaim, who dared an instant's teasing grin. Aunt Yehudis scowled darkly, Rachel turned her back upon him, and Mama kept talking.

"Polish, yes," Mama agreed weakly. "Hannah has also learned some German from the book peddler. But to read and write? To learn Hebrew?"

Aunt Yehudis threw up her hands in exasperation.

"Do you think the little one sits in services at *shul* every Sabbath morning counting windows? Or staring at the silver embroidery on the cushion before the Ark? Does she fall asleep upon her mother's shoulder? On Sabbath afternoons, who prompts Chaim and Muni, even Leibel, when their papa asks them questions about their studies?"

Mama did not answer directly. She only stammered.

"How—how shall I do without Hannah in this house?"

"Are you so feeble, you and Rachel, that you need the child to do your scrubbing? God forbid you should ask her to do your *mending*! I have watched her make hen tracks with her needle."

"B-but," Mama stammered a last time, "who is to *pay* Reb Doddl for his teaching?"

This time Aunt Yehudis turned fiery red. "I will pay, Rifka."

Then she and Mama began talking at once and together so that their words interlaced.

"You already have enough burdens, Yehudis. How can you afford this? You need all the money you earn."

"I tell you, I have my needle, and Reb Doddl has ten children. His wife's a pious woman but no seamstress. She cannot keep them all in clothes."

"Still, Yehudis, there's your poor crippled Nahum."

"Is my husband a heartless monster just because a cart fell upon him when he was young? You must let me do this, Rifka. We can pay for Hannah's schooling, since we have no little ones of our own. It is settled?"

"Yes, it—it is settled."

"Then God be praised!"

As Hannah stood in confusion, the two women began to wipe each other's tear-damp cheeks with their long black skirts until suddenly Aunt Yehudis gave a piercing cry.

"Oy, oy!"

"God help us! What is it, Yehudis?"

"Your soup, Rifka! The kettle is running over! Here we have the River Jordan itself!"

After the cover had been lifted from the gurgling kettle, and the soup wiped up from the floor, Aunt Yehudis turned, satisfied, to the door. "I must go home now. My Nahum is waiting for me. He does not go to *shul,* Rifka. You know that. He reads his newspapers and wants me there."

Only when she was out of sight did Muni dare to say, with a grimace, "Why do you want to go to school, Hannah?"

Chaim seconded him with an owlish pucker. "I should like to sit at home like a girl."

"*Sit* at home like a girl!" Rachel exclaimed from the far side of the supper table. "Ho! Boys should sit so much!"

"You must not speak so to your brother, Rachel." Mama silenced the argument. She shooed the boys and Papa, newly arrived after delivering a prayer shawl, off to the bath house, and then away to the services at *shul.* As soon as she and Rachel completed the Sabbath table, they washed themselves carefully from a basin, and Mama adjusted her Sabbath wig and her pearls. By the time the men's returning footsteps sounded in the street, Mama had also scrubbed Hannah and dressed her in her best clean clothes.

"You must not be surprised to see me look so fine. I have reason," Hannah told the two pale-faced, stoop-shouldered students whom Papa—as was his custom, even when the soup had boiled low—had brought home to share the Sabbath supper. "I am to go to school!"

It was not fitting, she knew, for a girl and the smallest child to speak so to Papa's guests. But she could not hold back the news and boldly repeated her words.

"I am to go to school. It is decided. Aaron has his violin, and I am to be a pupil at Reb Doddl's school."

Reb Doddl, Hannah soon discovered, was a stern schoolmaster, not like Muni's wretched young teacher. He bashed his pupils' heads together when they neglected their lessons, and he even beat boys who bullied their fellows or disrupted the class. The parents of the youngest boys left them with him in fear and trembling, slipping sweetmeats into the little ones' pockets to bribe them to be brave.

But everyone respected Reb Doddl. He was a learned man and, Papa said, if he had not stammered so badly, he might well have been a rabbi. He was also just. Best of all, Hannah saw, he had a high regard for girls. That was fortunate for him, since, of his ten thin-cheeked, big-eyed children, eight were daughters. It was fortunate for Hannah, also. He was kind to her at once and spent extra time with her so that she quickly caught up with the older boys and did not have to sit with the youngest pupils. All in all, it turned out that Aunt Yehudis had been right. Hannah was quick at book learning. Reb Doddl's school was a happy adventure.

In fact, it was an adventure just to cross the *shtetl* to her studies, for Mama would not, of course, let a seven-year-old go such a bewildering distance alone. It would be easy for her to get lost, Mama said. Besides, too many strangers wandered through the *shtetl*. They were not to be trusted. And then there were always peasant boys eager to pick fights with Jewish children.

Sometimes the twins took Hannah, Chaim walking on one side, Leibel on the other carrying her book bag. At Leibel's insistence they all went carefully down the middle of the streets so that they could see clearly any menace that might come from either right or left. In truth, except for the slippery ice and snow underfoot in winter and the blowing dust on dry, hot days, Hannah could see none of the dangers that Mama feared.

Less often, Muni was assigned to go with her, and then the trip was different. Muni was only ten, not yet as tall and strong-looking as his older brothers, but he raced along with his fierce Crusader's nose lifted high. She could scarcely keep up with him. Whenever any strange boys came near, Muni shouted warnings. "Stay away from my sister! You'll be sorry if you don't!"

If the boys did not back away at once, he picked up whatever lay in the street—sticks, stones, bits of garbage—and threw those missiles at them. Sticks and stones came back, of course, but for the most part, the bullies' aim was poor. Or perhaps they did not truly want to fight. Perhaps Muni only imagined their evil intentions.

One afternoon, however, when he had promised to fetch her from school, he did not appear. "He has forgotten me," Hannah told herself. "I must go home alone."

Although the *shtetl* streets were long and snaked around many corners, by now she had walked them often. Unlike Mama, always so cautious, she was sure that she could find her way. After the first tentative steps, she found it pleasant to choose her own pace, to pause when she wanted to stare at strangers' gabled houses and the church with its gilded cross and a priest in stiff bright vestments coming out of the door.

As she was rounding the corner past the church, she confronted a peasant boy, staring open-mouthed at her—a tiny Jewish girl with flaming red curls and a book bag dragging in the dust! Always before, one of her brothers had carried the bag for her. Defiantly, she hitched it up onto her shoulder.

But the boy advanced, his staring eyes blue and pale. All at once, he gave a quick bullfrog jump and reached for her hair.

"Carrot-top! Carrot-top!" he taunted.

Hannah was too swift for him, however. She ducked away from his grasp, stuck out her tongue, and stamped fiercely.

"If you touch me, I will poke out your eyes!" she threatened.

Pale lids blinking in surprise, the boy backed away from her, step by step. Then, all at once, he ran.

He had vanished around the shelter of the church wall when Hannah saw Muni limping down the street toward her. There was blood on his pants leg and his fists.

"Muni, Muni! What has happened to you?"

"Three boys jumped me." Muni gave a dry, wracking sob. "Th-they will not do it again, I can tell you."

"But the blood? Your leg?"

"We must go to the river and wash off the blood before we go home. By then I will not be limping badly."

Walks to and from school with Muni were exciting, though Hannah never told Mama about them. Still it was the trips with Aaron that were her true delight.

Aaron was out of school, nearly sixteen now, and so tall and strong and long-legged that he never tried to match his step to hers but carried her, high and secure, on his shoulders. Seeming never to have any fear of attacks, he walked the streets with the proud gait of a prince.

Hannah often saw passersby look at him admiringly, even move silently out of his path. The teenage girls, both Jewish and Gentile, giggled and blushed and straightened their flying hair. In spite of his grave, courteous smile, Aaron was not thinking about any of them. Even as he walked, he was immersed in his music.

Sometimes Hannah heard him humming or whistling and did not interrupt, for the melodies were so wonderfully sweet. Sometimes he stopped, shaking his head as if in surprise.

"I cannot help myself, *maidele,*" he would murmur. "The

music never stops sounding in my head." Then one day he added, "Now that I have finished studies at our *heder,* Papa is sad that he has not enough money to send me away to get more learning at a *yeshiva.* I am glad! I want to live only for my violin. Papa says in that case I will starve to death, but he is wrong. Someday you will all see. I shall be a great musician."

For an instant a longing, sharp and unbidden, stung Hannah's throat.

"When you are rich and famous, you must teach me to play the violin, too," she whispered.

Aaron did not hear her. He had begun to whistle, loud and clear, the Chopin mazurka. In the street people turned to listen. And Hannah laid her bright head against his dark one and was, in spite of her own longing, happy for this moment in his dream.

Rachel and Aaron

Unexpectedly it was Rachel, the eldest, the practical daughter, who caused the first spoken distress in the Eliashov family, the first bitter weeping and change in the family ways. That change began late one autumn day—a year after the beginning of Hannah's schooling—when Rachel came home from the market to announce that she and Moishe the Drayman were engaged. No need of a marriage broker for them, Rachel declared proudly. They had chosen each other, and by themselves.

Hannah was so excited at the news that she flew to her sister and gave her a warm hug and kiss.

"Mazel tov, Rachel! Good luck!" Then she flew over to Rachel's tall, broadly smiling fiancé. *"Mazel tov,* Moishe!"

As she looked away from Moishe's enormous height, she saw to her surprise that on the far side of the kitchen her parents stood stiffly, lips trembling. Mama's eyes welled with tears. Papa laid a hand on Mama's arm as if to silence and comfort her, and he himself looked strangely confused.

"You must give your parents time to think about this, Rachel. You must give us time, Moishe," he said haltingly. "The matter of a marriage is not decided in a moment."

57

"In a *moment*! Is that what he thinks of me?" Rachel demanded that night, as the two sisters lay side by side in their big curtained bed. "I have loved Moishe for a year!" But from the far side of the room, Hannah heard Mama weeping.

"A girl like our Rachel!" Mama sobbed. "With such beautiful eyes! Such a fine character! And an innkeeper's grandchild. A scholar's daughter. To marry a drayman, an ignoramus. A poor man, to boot. You must forbid it, Zavel."

Papa forbid one of his children? Papa, a man so gentle that he could hardly bring himself to shoo a peasant's suckling pig from the beets in the garden! Hannah heard Papa whispering now.

"Our Rachel is eighteen, a big girl, Rifka. We would not wish her to be an old maid. And then, times are changing. We are in the twentieth century now. Parents no longer make all the decisions for their children. This may even be for the best."

"It *may* be for the best?" Rachel's indignation swelled into Hannah's ear. "How else will I get a husband? A girl must face the truth. Are my eyes so beautiful that Aaron Itzak, the fur merchant's son, would take me without a dowry? Is my character so fine that the rabbi's son would choose me, though I am penniless and have no learning? As for learning, does all Papa's knowledge of the Talmud help him at his loom?

"Oh, but God forgive me," the older sister moaned as she turned her cheek passionately into the bed covers. "I do not mean to speak badly of Papa. Only, they *must* let me marry Moishe. It is not just that I must have a husband. I have told them, I *love* Moishe. If I were the richest, most beautiful girl in the *shtetl,* I would love him still!"

The next day, when Aunt Yehudis heard the news, she nodded sagely.

"We should have expected this. Rachel is not a girl to stand in the marketplace flirting idly with a stranger. She must have had her eyes on the drayman from the start. At all events, there's nothing to be done now. You know the saying, Rifka. It is harder to guard a girl in love than to guard a bagful of fleas."

With all her wisdom, however, Aunt Yehudis could not stop the deep division within the Eliashov family. Day followed day, and Papa did not give his blessing. Rachel began openly, stubbornly sewing her wedding dress, fiercely defying Mama to deny her the length of fine cloth that had been set aside years ago for this purpose. Despite all that defiance, Rachel's eyes were red with the tears she shed in the night, her heart bitter at having her beloved so rejected.

As for herself, Hannah liked Moishe more and more each day. It was true she would not have chosen him for a husband. He seemed to have little learning, and he knew no Hebrew. When Papa asked his sons questions about their studies on Sabbath afternoons, Moishe sat at Rachel's side, wordless and restless. He looked, Hannah thought, as if he heard a fly buzzing somewhere in the house but could not locate it and was waiting anxiously to see where it would alight.

Yet he was endlessly helpful and cheerful. On weekdays, when he came to the house, he would lift Hannah with one arm straight up above his head, as though she weighed no more than a baby. Once, when Chaim and Muni were wrestling too close to Papa's loom, he turned them both upon their backs with a simple turn of his wrist. They might have been turnips.

He was a giant truly, this Moishe Kopsofsky, half a head taller than any of the tall Eliashovs, with a great crop of thick golden hair. But with all his strength, he was as good-natured as a puppy, forever teasing and joking. You could hear his voice when he came near in the street.

Moishe never seemed to hold it against Mama and Papa that they did not yet accept him as Rachel's fiancé. With all his joking and high spirits, he always spoke respectfully to them. He treated their daughter as though she were a queen.

Yet the December night came when the wedding dress was finished, and still no consent to the marriage had been given, no plans made.

"It is as though Mama and Papa had stopped thinking of me!" Rachel cried bitterly into her pillow. "Are Moishe and I children who will soon forget what we have asked?"

Hannah reached out a hand in the darkness to comfort her sister, but Rachel flung it aside.

"I will not let them deny me any longer!" she declared. "You must be witness to what I say, Hannah. Tomorrow I will demand their permission. I will demand that Papa set a date!"

"Tomorrow? But that is the Sabbath. Would you truly dare—on the Sabbath, Rachel?"

"Perhaps God will hear me on that day!"

Alas, Rachel was to have no chance to speak.

She slept late that morning, exhausted by her sorrow, but

Hannah wakened early. Snow had fallen during the night. She could see a silvery rime through the narrow window beside her bed. With a little shiver, she slid deeper into the goose-down covers.

Then, quite suddenly, she heard a loud shouting and stamping in the street. Next came a violent hammering at the kitchen door. The house itself seemed to tremble.

There is a fire in the *shtetl,* Hannah thought, trembling, or robbers! Or a *pogrom,* more destroyers come to sweep us all out into the street!

Heart pounding, she jumped out of bed, wakened Rachel with a shake of her shoulder, and rushed into the kitchen. There she found Papa and the four boys stopped on their way to *shul* by soldiers blocking the doorway.

Snow glistened on the soldiers' beards and shoulders, and on the long, shining barrels of their rifles. They wasted no words. They had come for Aaron, the oldest son in the family, they announced curtly. Aaron was to be a conscript in the Tsar's army.

Their purpose announced, the soldiers glared threateningly around at the dazed, open-mouthed family. Only the youngest of them, a dull-eyed peasant boy, round-faced, flat-featured, hardly as old as Aaron himself, looked away out the window, pulling nervously at his earlobe as though he did not like his job. But, at his officer's command, he too sprang about sharply.

"Time to move on, Jew!" The boy jerked at Aaron's shoulder, prodded him in the ribs with his rifle butt.

"You must not do that!" Hannah could no longer keep

silent. In a burning fountain, words leaped from her throat. "You must not hurt my brother!"

She flew toward the young soldier, arms flailing, but the boy jabbed his elbow at her. The blow drove the breath from her chest, and she fell backward.

"See! They have bayonets! They could stab you through!" Rachel cried, as she caught her sister in her arms.

"But th-they will h-hurt him! They m-must not!"

It was Papa's voice that came to her then, heavy and hopeless.

"The Tsar is the law, *maidele.* We cannot disobey his soldiers. They will not hurt Aaron if he goes with them peaceably. They want his health and strength. We will only make his life harder if we resist them." Papa bowed his head humbly, a beaten child.

If I were a man, I would not do that! I would fight them, Hannah thought desperately. Her gaze flashed toward Muni, standing on the far side of the kitchen, crimson to the temples, savagely chewing his lips. Surely Muni would attack his brother's captors.

But he did not. His dark eyes turned to Papa, and a terrible helplessness coursed across his face.

Aaron alone stood proud and unflinching. All at once, as Hannah watched him, his mouth puckered and, even while the soldier boy roughly whirled him about toward the door, he began to whistle.

It was the mazurka! Chopin's dauntless mazurka, the melody with the graceful repeated notes and the sudden thrust toward the stars!

After that bold sound, everything else happened swiftly.

Papa stumbled to the door to take his eldest son in his arms for one last time. Mama followed, sobbing loudly. "Be good, my eldest son. Live Torah!"

Then, ordering Aaron before them, the soldiers stomped away down the cold street. The white flakes they had brought into the house on their boots, which at first had looked like flower petals, now melted into savage black footprints on the kitchen floor.

That evening, Aunt Yehudis came with news of why the soldiers had arrived without warning. It was Aaron Itzak, the fur merchant's son, whose name had been on the army conscription list. But Reb Itzak had given the soldiers a bagful of *zlotys* not to carry off his boy. He had bribed them to take instead Aaron, the son of Zavel, the weaver, a poor man.

"I hate Reb Itzak!" cried Chaim, for once in his life fierce and furious. "I will break every window in his house!"

"I hate Reb Itzak's Aaron!" stormed Muni. "I'll knock him to the ground and stomp on him, that one who wears fur mitts when we shiver, who has apples and nuts spilling out of his pockets while others go hungry. I'll break every bone in his fat body!"

But Papa shook his head.

"You will not do that, Muni. Violence is not our way."

"But, Papa, Reb Itzak—"

"With such a poor, sickly wife, the fur merchant has only one child. In his place, if I had had a bagful of money to buy my son's freedom and let another's be taken, I might have acted as he did. God forgive me, I might have done it. Reb Itzak is not an evil man."

Papa fell silent, while Aunt Yehudis tried to wipe Mama's streaming cheeks.

For days after Aaron's going, all of the Eliashovs, even Muni, walked about numbly, not speaking, scarcely touching food. In fact, there would have been no food prepared had it not been for Rachel—Mama had given herself up to grief.

"We are ghosts!" she sobbed night and morning. "This is what it is like to be dead." Or, "My poor Aaron! My eldest son! The army has taken him away for twenty-five years. I shall never see him again."

Finally, after weeks of such wailing, Aunt Yehudis paid her sister a visit to protest.

"You must stop crying, Rifka. It is good to cry out new sorrow. For a day or so, yes. For a week. But a month and more? It is a scandal! A disgrace! Your Aaron's no dummy. Don't you think he will find a way to escape from the Tsar's army?"

Hannah herself had not thought of that. Although she stood close beside Mama, patting her arm, she looked questioningly toward Papa. He was nodding.

"Listen to your sister, Rifka. She may be right. When I was a boy, I had a good friend named Simon. The soldiers conscripted his whole class at the *yeshiva,* but Simon escaped from the regiment. The soldiers never found him. In the end, he made his way across Poland and took ship for America. The Tsar's power does not reach to America. There, they say, even a Jew is free."

"Why should our Aaron not escape, then?" Aunt Yehudis nodded the more fiercely with each word. "He is strong, that one. Aaron could walk to Siberia, pushing this house before him. I promise you, Rifka, he's not fated like some poor fellows to carry a gun for twenty-five years and forget his people. The next news you receive of him may be a letter from New York."

But Mama went on sobbing. "My son, my son. Are you all monsters that you do not weep for him, too?"

Then, unexpectedly, the unhappiness that had built up in Rachel even before Aaron's going, as well as the unhappiness of his loss and her own long hours of cooking, cleaning, and washing for the family—all of her misery broke out cruelly.

"Hear Mama cry for her Aaron!" Rachel mocked when Aunt Yehudis had left the house. "Does the woman have no son left to pray for her when she dies? Listen to her sob. She has forgotten all the rest of her children. She thinks of one only. She is not a true mother to six. We shall all of us be lost!"

These words did what Aunt Yehudis's and Papa's anxious appeals had not brought about. Mama abruptly stopped crying. The next morning, she cooked breakfast for the first time in weeks. Then she went to the bedroom, emerging with her thick shawl wrapped around her head and body and a bag in her hand. The treasure box lay open on the bed behind her.

"She is going to the pawnbroker," Hannah whispered to Rachel.

But why? What good was money to any of them now? That mystery was solved at noontime, when Mama returned, her head held high, her face white and dry as paper. Boldly, she marched to Rachel's side.

"You are to be married at once, you and your Moishe," she commanded and held out a fat leather purse. "Take this money and buy steamship tickets."

"Married? Steamship tickets?"

Unbelieving and astonished, Rachel was not even able to hold out her hands. Sternly, Mama thrust the leather purse into the pocket of her daughter's underskirt.

"You must obey your mama. You and Moishe are to go to Ellis Island. To America," she ordered.

"America!" Hannah gasped. For a long moment, Rachel stood as if chained to the floor. Then she shook her head wildly.

"Oh, Mama, you must forgive my harsh words last night. I cannot accept such a sacrifice. You have pawned your dearest treasures. Your gold pin. The ring with the blue stone like a flower. The comb of tortoiseshell. I saw—they are all of them missing from your box."

"Baubles, baubles!" Mama patted Rachel's hand. "My treasures, you call them. I tell you, they are nothing. It is our dear ones who are important. Your Moishe must never be taken away to be a soldier. Nor my young sons, either. Like your papa's friend Simon, Moishe will be free and safe in America, and you two will send back money for more steamship tickets. For Chaim and Leibel, for Muni, too, when he is older. This you must promise me."

So there was, after all, a wedding in the Eliashov family late that winter. Rachel glowed like a princess when, dressed in the beautiful gown into which she had put so many resolute stitches, she went under the canopy with Moishe for the ceremony. After the promises had been made and the wineglass shattered, a feast was served and the fiddler played his songs. For a few hours, everyone was joyous once again.

Then, on an icy morning one week later, the newlyweds went to board the long, steam-wreathed train that would carry them across Poland to Warsaw and, in time, still farther to the port city of Antwerp on the shores of the Atlantic Ocean. There they would find the immigrant ship that would carry them the unknowable distance to America, to Ellis Island and freedom from the Tsar's soldiers.

On the station platform, Rachel held Hannah close in a last, long embrace.

"I shall be your big sister forever, *maidele*. Remember me," she whispered.

"Remember me, too," said giant Moishe with a grin.

But this morning, Hannah could not return his smile. Instead, she squeezed her eyes tightly shut. When she opened them and could once again see clearly, the train had drawn out of the station and, scarcely larger now than a pebble, was rolling away down the narrowing tracks.

Aunt Yehudis touched a soothing hand to her cheek.

"Why so woebegone, *maidele*? Our Rachel and Moishe are young and strong. They will be welcomed at Ellis Island. They will be happy," she declared.

Chaim and Leibel ⟐

Now, her loneliness doubled, Hannah turned to a long-forbidden comfort. Aaron's violin.

At first she only dreamed of touching it late at night as she lay in her newly spacious bed. One day, however, she boldly brought it down from the loft and laid it upon the kitchen table. To her surprise, Mama did not object.

Mama had not wept since Rachel's departure. It was as if she had no more tears to shed. Instead, she seemed somehow to be waiting, waiting for something that had not yet arrived.

"Take good care of the violin, *maidele*," she said abstractedly to Hannah and turned her head away.

Nor did Mama offer any help or instruction when her daughter took the precious instrument from its case and touched the bow to the strings. But Hannah had listened so often, so intently, to Aaron's lessons that it seemed to her she scarcely needed Mama's instruction. She needed only the chance to play.

She did not have much free time, it was true. She had become one of Reb Doddl's best pupils, and she did not wish to stop learning. Reb Doddl would have been deeply disappointed. Papa, too. Though he did not put his feelings into words, Papa was clearly proud to have found a student in his youngest child.

In addition to her schooling, Hannah had to spend many hours a week helping Mama. Mama was always distressed when her home was not tidy and glistening, and she was used to Rachel's capable assistance. In her strange, waiting mood she could not care for her house and family alone.

There were bright spring afternoons, when the breeze seemed to carry away all the harsh smells of the *shtetl* and flowers bloomed bright as jewels in window pots. On these precious occasions, Hannah would steal out for a few moments to play with the neighborhood children.

Such moments were not frequent, of course, and Mama, raised in her fine inn with the children of scholars and musicians for her friends, had never approved of her daughters playing with anyone who might pass in the street. When the family had been together, Hannah had not thought of arguing, since she had found all the companionship she wanted with her brothers and sister. Now her dearest companion was her violin.

For a time she was awkward with it and discouraged that she made only squawks when moving the bow across the strings. Yet, she remembered, Aaron had also been awkward at first. Within a few weeks she was playing scales and melodies she had heard from him. To her surprise and delight, she found these were all safely stored in her memory. She was certain that her pitch was true.

Though Papa could not tell one song from another, he was pleased to see her happy, and he smiled encouragement from his corner of the kitchen. Leibel smiled also.

The other boys and Mama paid little attention. Mama was waiting, waiting—she confessed, in time—for a letter from Rachel.

No letters came, though spring had passed, as well as summer and fall, and a new winter had begun.

"Would we hear if Rachel's ship had gone down at sea?" asked Leibel anxiously. "How long does it take to cross the Atlantic?"

"She has vanished, your eldest," said the Eliashovs' next-door neighbor. "It happens to many of them. They go away over the seas to America and roll up the pathway behind them. They grow rich and forget their poor families in the *shtetl.*"

"Oy, oy, oy! That neighbor of yours, Rifka! What a gloomy one!" Aunt Yehudis mocked. "Do not listen to her. She expects every kettle to leak."

The first message came at last—a short one.

Dearest Family,
Our voyage was a stormy one, but we arrived safely in New York last week. We have rented a room with kind friends we met on the ship. There are six of us here. Moishe is looking for work. We both send our love,

Your Rachel

After that note, there was no more news from America. Her sister had never been one for writing, Hannah reminded herself. Rachel had been too busy helping Mama with the house and with the younger children to have had time for study. For her, writing a letter would be hard.

Then came the fateful envelope. From "Pittsburgh, Pennsylvania," Papa read. "Though who has heard of such a place?" The family, with Aunt Yehudis among them, all gathered around the supper table to stare at the contents of the envelope, which fell out into Papa's lap. There was a short letter penciled in Rachel's cramped hand. And a steamship ticket!

"A year and a few months only have passed, and Rachel sends a steamship ticket!" Aunt Yehudis exclaimed in wonder. "America is truly the Golden Land!"

"About golden lands I don't know." A little furrow creased Papa's brow. "Rachel says Moishe decided it would be easier to find steady work in Pittsburgh than in New York. The city is not so large, and people are friendly. She sends us her love and says she and Moishe are well, but she does not speak of gold. And there is only one ticket."

"One ticket will not take both the twins," Mama said, frowning.

There was a family council meeting which lasted far into the night. In the end, Mama and Papa decided that Chaim must use the steamship ticket, since he had always been the bolder and stronger of the two. Chaim's owlish smile faded, and he protested at having to leave his brother. "We have never been apart for an hour." But even he was forced to agree that he was the more likely to find work at once.

Of course, Chaim could not go penniless or empty-handed. "At Ellis Island they demand that a boy be strong and healthy, with money to support himself until he can earn more," Aunt Yehudis declared with her usual assurance. This time Mama would be obliged to sell the last treasures from her jewel box. The golden belt clasp, the pearls.

With the money paid by the pawnbroker, Mama bought Chaim a new wicker suitcase, food, and warm clothing for the journey. She wrote letters asking distant cousins in Warsaw to give lodging to her boy while he waited there for his visa. In the lining of his suitcase, she hid the money that would assure him entry at Ellis Island.

On the departure day, Leibel carried his brother's luggage to the railroad station. The rest of the family tried to chatter happily as they stood upon the station platform, watching the train show its black nose in the distance and then come rushing threateningly toward them. The twins themselves stood silent, holding stubbornly to each other until the warning whistle sounded.

For an instant, Hannah almost thought that Chaim would not put his foot on the step. But Mama, with surprising strength, urged him up into the car.

"Be a good boy, Chaim. Live Torah. Say your prayers," she admonished him. *"And send quickly for your brother."*

Mama's last command was obeyed. First came a brief note saying that Chaim was safe in Pittsburgh. Five months later, a second steamship ticket arrived with an urgent letter.

"Our Chaim has turned thief!" Aunt Yehudis exclaimed. "Even in America a boy could not earn enough money to buy a ticket so quickly."

But Chaim, as he explained, had *not* turned thief. Although he was the stronger and bolder twin, he had always depended, more than even he himself had guessed, upon Leibel's care. He wrote:

> I am so lonely you would not know me. I do not know myself. I am like a wool coat shrunk by rain. So I have borrowed the money to bring Leibel to me. The interest rate is high, but together we will pay back the money.
>
> We cannot ask more of Rachel. She and Moishe are well, and kind to me, but they have not found riches. He works very hard. They would not have room for two of us. Soon they will not even have room for me. Leibel and I will go to Youngstown, Ohio. You will not have heard of Youngstown, but there are shirt factories in that city. We will surely find jobs.
>
> I am waiting for my brother. He must come at once.
>
> *Chaim*

And now a new threat descended, a threat that Hannah had not foreseen.

"In so few months, we have had no time to save the many *zlotys* Leibel must show when he arrives at Ellis Island. One solution only is possible," Mama declared. "We must sell the violin."

"The *violin*? Oh, no! No, you cannot!" Hannah protested. "I would—Aaron would—Aaron will need it one day!"

"Pray God for that day, but it will not come tomorrow. For now, we must save Leibel."

"But, Mama, Mama, you must not sell the violin! Papa, tell her—"

It was Leibel who touched Hannah's burning cheek, smoothed her hair.

"Hannah is right, Mama," he murmured. "You must not sell Aaron's violin. It is precious to him.

"There is something more to be said. What will you and Papa do without me? Who will watch over you all? It is true that I am lonely for Chaim. I am always listening for his footsteps. But my brother has reached the Golden Land. He is clever. He will make his way. And you need me here."

"You are too good, Leibel! You always were," cried Mama. "But you must not let us hold you back."

"Listen to your son, Mama. I do not want to go away. I am content in the *shtetl*. In a few years—three or four at the most—Muni will go to America in my place. Chaim and Muni together will become rich men. As for me, I will be happy to stay with you here."

But Mama would not be convinced. Her fine dark eyes were flaming.

"Zavel, tell the boy, we will not let a son throw away his life."

The argument lasted for many days. Not since Rachel had first brought Moishe home had there been such a battle. Hannah listened to the angry voices in terror.

Though her heart ached at seeing the family become like a tree struck by frost, all its beautiful leaves flying, she had known for a long time that her brothers must leave the *shtetl*. Mama would not be turned from that resolve. But the *violin*! How could she live without it?

As for Leibel, his misery seemed quite as great as her own.

"They do not love me," he sighed brokenly after the bitterest of the quarrels. They were alone, for Mama had gone to market, Muni had plunged away into the street, and Papa also had left the house. There were times when Papa, though a patient man, could no longer bear the tedium of the loom and needed to seek companions, the rabbi and others with whom he could talk of the Talmud and the scriptures he loved.

"Mama and Papa do not love me," Leibel repeated, hugging his long, thin arms across his chest. "If they loved me, they would not want to send me so far away."

"You know that is not true," Hannah said, shaking her head. "You can't think they will be happy without you. It is only because they *do* love you that they want to make sure you will never be one of the Tsar's soldiers. Oh, but, Leibel, there is something else." She stopped abruptly, fighting her tears.

"What is it *maidele*? You look so unhappy."

"It—it is the violin." She lifted her face. "Now that I am losing you all, the violin is my dearest friend. You know that, Leibel. I dream—" she had scarcely known this herself, but the words came startlingly, unbidden. "I even dream that someday I will be a musician. Like the fiddler. Like Aaron."

"And so you shall, *maidele*!" After a long pause, swallowing hard, Leibel said, "I will always help you in any way I can. You have my promise. To begin with, I will tell Mama and Papa that I will never go to America if they sell the violin. They must keep it forever. For Aaron—and for you."

"Oh, thank you, Leibel." Hannah caught his hand. "But will they find the money to send you?"

"I—I think Papa has found a way."

And Leibel was right. That evening, Papa stepped into the kitchen, shut the door carefully behind him, and drew a jingling bag from beneath the flap of his coat.

"What do you have there, Zavel?" Mama demanded, whirling about from the stove.

"Money to let Leibel in at Ellis Island. To let Chaim pay back his debt. It is decided now. Leibel will do as I tell him. He will go to the Golden Land."

Mama gave a low cry and threw her skirt over her face. Muni, who had come home only moments before, his clothes soiled and darkened with river water—did Mama never notice those telltale stains, Hannah wondered—shouted triumphantly. Leibel himself, saying nothing, bent his head.

"But where did he get the money?" Muni whispered urgently after the brothers, Hannah with them, had crept up to the loft. Downstairs, Mama and Papa had begun emptying out the *zlotys* and making final plans for the journey. "Where did he get so much? If I knew, I would get more and go with you, Leibel."

"It was n–not the v–violin," Hannah stammered, her heart beating hard. "Papa has realized now how much the violin means to me."

"Ho! That old instrument would not have brought half so much money," Muni scoffed. "Do you know where he got it, Leibel?"

"I think I do. Yes." Leibel nodded hesitantly. "Poor

Papa. With all his pride. I saw him, only yesterday, going into Reb Itzak's house. He did not notice that I was passing on the other side of the street."

"Reb Itzak's house?"

"I believe Papa decided at last to ask Reb Itzak to help one of *his* sons."

Muni shook his head savagely. With the loss of his brothers, Muni always seemed like a cock fighting the bars of a cage. "I don't understand you."

But Hannah did. The thought came to her suddenly and clearly, although her gratitude to Papa was so blended with pity and love for him that she could explain only haltingly.

"Oh, Muni, you must see. Reb Itzak is a rich man, but he is not a bad one. Papa said that. All this time, the fur merchant must have felt guilty for giving the bribe that sent away our Aaron. Papa counted on that guilt and turned to Reb Itzak for help. He has got it now."

"And if Papa cared so much and Reb Itzak was willing," Leibel declared softly, "it must be that I was meant to go away."

So many days later, the next Eliashov traveler boarded the train to Warsaw, as had his brother and sister. As he climbed the steps, Mama's old wicker suitcase bumped against his long, thin legs. It was the last luggage in the family and contained a meager weight of bread and cheese, carefully patched clothing, and, in the tattered lining beneath the clothing, the money so astonishingly gained.

Hannah, from the station platform, saw Leibel stare longingly at the case as though it hid not such a slight treasure but all the good memories of his life. Only as the train whistle sounded departure did he look up, past the travelers crowding around him, to raise a trembling hand in farewell.

Several long days later, Leibel climbed off a last train, this one having brought him to Antwerp. He clutched his bag anxiously, trying to fight back tears of bewilderment and despair.

"You are not well, boy?" A man's voice came abruptly out of the jostling crowd. "You look confused. What is wrong?"

"N-no, n-nothing," Leibel murmured unsteadily. "It is only—only that I must find myself a room for the night. A cheap room. And I do not know where to look."

"I must find myself a room, also." The man nodded encouragement. "I know a hostel nearby. You are welcome to come with me. I think you must be a stranger in Antwerp."

"Oh, yes."

"Hold fast to your suitcase then. Watch your pockets. Among so many strangers, there are always some you can't trust. Come along. Stay close beside me."

Never in his life had Leibel been in a throng like the one that filled the streets of Belgium's great port city. In the *shtetl,* a crowd had been ten—twenty—at the most, a knot of folks in the market, or a Sabbath congregation at *shul.* Here, he could not count the people who surrounded him. Nor was the throng made up only of people. There were horse-drawn carriages and huge, freight-laden carts, each wheel as big as the biggest mill wheels at home.

Some people darted here and there through the traffic, as confident as salamanders in water. But others made their way cautiously. Still others—men, women, and children in *shtetl* garments, newly arrived from the east—stood as if paralyzed and did not move at all.

"Poor things! They, too, wish they had never left home," Leibel sighed aloud. "I wish that I could comfort them." But his new friend beckoned him onward and continued to move rapidly through the crowd.

Reaching the safety of the hostel and a tiny, windowless room beneath the eaves was a kind of miracle. Although the air in the cramped space was stale, Leibel breathed deeply.

"You should know," he assured his companion, "that my name is Leibel Eliashov. You will not be sorry that you helped me. I can be trusted."

"I believe you." The stranger gave an amused smile. "You mean to stop over for some time in Antwerp?"

"No, I shall board a steamship very soon. I am on my way to America."

"I thought as much."

"You, too, are on your way to America?"

"No, my trip takes me only to Antwerp. I have a large family, you see, many responsibilities, and little money. I am a doctor, a very poor doctor who is often not paid his fees."

Leibel frowned. "I, too, thought I should stay at home. But Mama and Papa say that going to America is the best way to help my family. Do you think they are right?"

The doctor smiled once again, comfortingly. "I agree with your parents. From the look of you, I can tell that they are good and wise people. I can tell also that they would very much want you to have a good, hot supper tonight."

"I *am* hungry . . . though I have bread and cheese in my suitcase," Leibel added hastily.

"You will be hungry enough for that bread and cheese later. Put your suitcase under the bed and come with me. I will take you to an inn I know well. Let's go quickly. We will soon be screaming at each other if we stay in this shabby closet all evening. See here, even the lock on the door is flimsy. Hurry. I am as hungry as you are."

So Leibel found himself again following the friendly doctor down Antwerp's streets. With the approach of night, the traffic had become lighter, the throng of people less densely packed, but the great freight-filled carts still rumbled toward the docks. Leibel himself felt faint. The long train ride and his fasting—for, in his anxiety, he had long been unable to eat— had affected him more than he had realized. Weak with hunger, he swayed a little and then jerked himself upright.

It was as the doctor looked back questioningly that Leibel noticed four people on the far side of the street. They were a father and mother and two lively children—a boy of seven or eight and a smaller girl with hair as flaming as Hannah's. All four wore the dark, heavy clothing of a *shtetl* family.

Above the street noises, no one could hear the family's voices, but Leibel could see that the parents were frightened of the traffic, while the children, unafraid, played with a red ball close to the passing vehicles. They seemed to delight in coming as close as possible to the rumbling wheels. Or maybe they were thinking only of their game.

In spite of his need to keep up with the doctor's quick pace, Leibel paused to watch the little girl. At that moment, the ball escaped from the child's hand and rolled into the middle of the street.

With a quick cry, the child came darting toward him in pursuit of her toy. Looking neither right nor left, she did not see the heavy freight cart bearing down upon her. Leibel himself must have more nearly sensed than seen the draft horses and the great turning wheels. Perhaps he was conscious only of an advancing shadow, like a dark wing of danger, when he flung himself forward, reached the girl, and, before he fell, pushed her mightily so that she went sliding back across the street.

Muni and Mama

The doctor was an honest man. He mailed the steamship ticket back to the Eliashovs.

Papa read his lengthy letter aloud to Mama, Hannah, and Aunt Yehudis. "It is in German and signed with a German name," he explained.

> You can be proud of your son. He died saving the life of another. It is said there is no greater love. I found Leibel's passport, with his name, his *shtetl* address, and the steamship ticket, pinned into the pocket of his shirt. He had also a suitcase. You will know that. He had said he had food, and there were no doubt clothes. I am sorry that I cannot send these things back to you, since they were stolen from the hostel room when we went out for supper.
>
> The room was easily broken into, I am afraid. Perhaps I should never have taken the lad under my wing. Sometimes we mean kindness and do harm. Forgive me.
>
> I am certain that your son was a noble boy.
>
> Respectfully,
> *Dr. Otto Wagner*

82

A deep stillness fell upon the house as Papa came to those last words. And now, as they had begun to do in the lonely days since Leibel's departure, even when they had believed him safe and happy, the family realized just how much they had owed to the gentle boy.

Since he had gone, the weeds in Mama's tiny garden had remained unpulled. There was never enough firewood in the box beside her stove. Papa's bobbins were always getting lost or tangled, rolling away across the kitchen floor or becoming hopelessly lost down the cracks between the boards. Papa's prayer books were forever getting misplaced. Leibel had been the one for keeping all these things in order.

As for Hannah, she could not believe the letter they had received.

"There could be a mistake," she insisted to Papa. "The doctor may not be an honest man. Or he could have found another boy run down in the street. For all we know, Leibel may be upon the high seas. Or even in New York."

In the end, when no further word came except a sad letter from Chaim, to whom Papa had written the news, Hannah was obliged to admit that Papa was right. Yet the admission was not an end. Rather, it was the start of a fresh Eliashov adventure.

It began one stormy evening when Muni came rushing home. As he flew through the kitchen door, his dark eyes glittering, he held up a bloody, swollen hand. "I am leaving the *shtetl*," he cried.

"You have been fighting again, Muni," Mama protested. She had known after all, then, that the stains of river water meant blood and dirt had been washed from her wild son's body and clothes. "Will you never *stop* fighting?"

"Not as long as I must stay in this cursed village. With my brothers gone, I must defend myself alone against the bullies who are always ready to fight. I have no chance against them.

"I will go to America in Leibel's place. He wanted me to go from the start. You all know that. I myself know something more. I will not go to this Pittsburgh, Pennsylvania, and become a poor peddler like Moishe. I will not go to this Youngstown, Ohio, and make shirts. I will stay in the great city of New York and become a rich man."

"How will you do that, Muni?" Hannah demanded, her eyes opening wide. Muni, with his passionate words, had cast a spell.

"I am not certain how, but I will find the road to riches. You need not doubt that. I will make money and buy a big house in New York with a roof whose tiles do not fly away in the wind and a stove that never goes out!"

Then Mama, with a quiet passion and Aunt Yehudis's support, tried to hold back the last of her boys.

"Perhaps I was wrong to force Leibel to leave us. As the doctor has written, sometimes we mean good and do harm.

"Wait a while, Muni. A year or two or three. You are too young to go alone, and the soldiers will not soon come to take you into the army. Wait, Muni. Your papa and Hannah and I need your help."

With each of his mother's pleas, Muni only shook his head more violently.

"I tell you, I'll not stay here any longer! Would you have me beaten every day because I do not bow down to the peasant boys? Would you have me be a putrid water carrier all the days of my life?"

"Your Papa was a water carrier, Muni, when the *pogroms* first drove us into the streets. That was no disgrace to him. But go to Bialystok if you will not stay in the *shtetl*," Mama went on pleading. "Your Papa has a cousin in Bialystok. It is not far away."

"That's a big town." Aunt Yehudis nodded. "They have unions of Jewish workers. Your Uncle Nahum reads about them in his newspapers. You'll find work there, get good wages. In a year or two or three, you'll have earned a fat purse."

Desperately, as Muni continued to shake his head ever more wildly, Mama went on. "They'll not let you into America without money, Muni. They'll not admit a beggar there. Aunt Yehudis says they'll want you to show them twenty-five dollars. She has checked on the sum. That is many *zlotys,* and we cannot give you as much as one coin. Your brother's suitcase was stolen with all the money. I have nothing else to pawn."

"A suitcase is a bother. Heavy to carry. Clothes are heavy, too. Who needs money?" Muni shouted.

He shouted, Hannah thought, because he was ashamed to be disobeying Mama and, in spite of himself, afraid of the journey, but still determined to go. "I tell you, I will fast till Ellis Island! I'll not need to eat at all!"

"And who will reward you for fasting?" demanded Aunt

Yehudis. "At Ellis Island they're not letting in beggars or scarecrows."

"Listen to me, Muni," begged Mama one last time. "Your mother begs you to wait. You will need a passport, a visa, money. To get all that takes time."

But that night, Muni slipped away while the others were sleeping, exhausted by their grief and their pleading. He left no note and took only the steamship ticket and the clothes he wore on his back. He did not take Aaron's violin, which Hannah found still in its place on the attic shelf.

Muni had always been a slammer of doors, a kicker of tables, a shouter. Although he was not yet full-grown, he took up a man's space.

When he was gone, sending no message after him, the house seemed like a sucked eggshell. For days, Hannah and Mama and Papa went about on tiptoes as if afraid to make a sound, even to cry. In the silence, Hannah could hear her own breath. When she played the violin, her only comfort, she crept upstairs to the loft.

Perhaps it was because they were all trying to hide so much sorrow from each other that none of the others noticed the early signs of Mama's illness. Aunt Yehudis said later that Mama must have known for a long time that the pains in her chest were serious. That was why she had hurried the boys away to safety, while she had time. Alone, Papa, who was so gentle, so soft-hearted, would never have found enough *zlotys* or mustered enough resolve to make all his sons leave him.

Whether Aunt Yehudis was right about that, Mama never said. What was certain was that she wrote no more letters to her children across the sea. Either she hadn't the strength or did not want to send bad news. Three months after Muni had slipped away into the night, she took to her bed. As she lay there between the heavy curtains, each breath she took seemed to pain her. She began to heave deep, rattling sighs.

During the first weeks of the illness, when one could hope that raspberry syrup, charms, and spells might work a cure, Hannah continued her studies with Reb Doddl. Those studies, at least, had not ended with the family departures, and, though books could never satisfy her as music did, they were still a joy.

But Mama grew worse. At last, Hannah was determined to make a sacrifice.

"I will no longer go to school. I will watch by Mama's bed."

Aunt Yehudis protested loudly. Then she wept. "Your mama would not ask for this. She would not wish it. She wants you to be a learned woman. I myself will be her nurse."

Papa also paced the house in distress. "This is too much to ask of you, *maidele*. Too much!"

Hannah defied them both. Even Reb Doddl's disappointment did not persuade her. She no longer crossed the *shtetl* each morning. Hour after hour, she stayed beside the sickbed. Sometimes she hummed a lullaby, sometimes the melodies that Aaron had played upon his violin. Sometimes, for fear of wakening the patient from rare moments of sleep, she sat rigid, making no sound at all, or she crept away to the loft to play softly to herself. Always, she prayed fiercely that Mama would be well.

When at last she saw that prayers—not only her own but Papa's and all those of the worshipers at *shul*—were not reaching God, she refused to eat.

Papa and Aunt Yehudis sternly forbade this fasting. They offered tempting food, bowls of chicken soup, bread and honey, blackberries fresh from the forest. Aunt Yehudis herself had gone out to pick the berries, a rare treat. Her skirt was dark with juice stains and heavy morning dew.

"You must eat, *liebchen,*" she commanded.

"Eat," Papa begged. "Life is precious. For a child, fasting is forbidden."

Despite her stomach pains, however, Hannah continued to defy them. Surely God would notice and reward her sacrifice. Surely He would make Mama well.

She waited for that happy day.

Then, one afternoon when she sat by her bedside, Mama awakened. Her eyes, opened wide, were no longer glazed with sickness. As in the old days before Aaron's leaving, they were like the petals of some beautiful, dark flower.

Mama thrust her hand out from beneath the coverlet. Her voice was strong and clear, like a bell.

"Promise me, Hannah, that you will take care of your papa as long as he needs you. You are all he has now."

"*All he has now?* Oh, Mama, I'll not let you go!" Hannah cried. "Of course, I will take care of Papa. I promise. But—"

"Ssh, *maidele.* There is one more thing you must do. Play

the violin here beside me. Play it now. Give me that pleasure."

"Oh, Mama, then—then you have heard me!"

"Heard you? Is your mama a deaf woman? Hurry, I cannot wait long."

And so Hannah, scarcely believing what she did, rushed away to the loft, brought down the violin, tuned it as best she could with her trembling fingers, and began to play. Song after song rushed from the strings. Her music filled the bedroom.

When at last she had finished, she saw Mama smile just once more.

"Beautiful, *maidele*. I am so proud of you," the white lips whispered. "There is much that you cannot teach yourself. The bowing, the vibrato, other things. For all that, one must have a teacher. But already you have the great thing— the soul."

Then Mama's eyes closed. Her hand, with the wedding ring tied to the thinned finger so that it would not slip away into the covers, sank down upon the bed. She sighed from somewhere unreachably far away.

It was four days after Mama's still body had been laid out with a candle at her head. It was three days after the long, twisting walk to the House of Graves. Papa and Hannah were still sitting *shiva,* mourning and receiving friends. On the far side of the Atlantic Ocean, Muni came at last to Ellis Island.

Muni's determination had carried him over land and water, but on this foggy morning in New York Harbor, despite his boldness, he again remembered Aunt Yehudis's mockery. "At Ellis Island they're not letting in beggars or scarecrows." He heard the distant echo of those words as he entered the great red immigration building.

Of some things, of course, he was certain. These foreign officials, with their probing eyes, could know nothing about his past that he did not choose to tell them. His passport added five years to his age, but, like all the Eliashov brothers, he was tall and strongly built, even if thinned by months of eating little. No one here could prove that he had lied about his birth date. Or that he had falsely claimed to be an orphan, as if somehow Mama and Papa could reach across the miles to stop his flight.

The officials could see, however, that he carried no luggage except the meager bundle thrown on his back. They could see that nowhere in his tattered clothing was there so much as a *zloty* to keep him while he looked for work. Worst of all, the tall, uniformed public health officer could see, when he turned back Muni's eyelids, what Muni himself had not realized.

"Trachoma. We do not let anyone come to America with such badly infected eyes. You must go back, Muni Eliashov."

"Go back?" Muni gasped.

"Many have been turned back before you. We must obey the law."

Helpless, Muni fell silent. If he had remained as bold as he had been at home in the *shtetl,* he would have stormed until he got his way or had no more breath in his body. He would have used his fists—even the one that was still badly scarred from his last battle in the *shtetl,* and had been injured again in a cruel scuffle on the dock at Antwerp, where he had been beaten for trying to steal a loaf of bread.

Here everything was different. In the huge immigration building, hemmed in by the long lines of men, women, and children desperately waiting their turn, confronted by so many officials with all the power of America at their command— here, even Muni's wild courage died. Of what use was it to fight? He would only be crushed as Leibel had been. The great wheel of fate was hard.

That night he stood on the moving deck of the ship to which he had been assigned, a ship bound back across the seas for England. Beyond the ship's stern, beyond the bubbling wake that she cut in the dark harbor waters, the lights of New York glittered. It was as though a thousand stars had fallen from the sky upon the rich island of Manhattan. Those stars spoke a brilliant and taunting good-bye.

In despair, Muni pounded his injured fist upon the ship's rail. A savage pain shot up his arm. All at once, he knew what he must do. One swift vault across the rail toward the water, and all his misery would be ended! One swift vault and then—

It was as he felt himself beginning to float above the water like a black bat in the darkness, his feet free of the ship's deck, and only the fingers of his left hand still touching the rail, that he heard the rush of a body behind him, felt viselike hands grasp his arm.

"Let me go! Let me go!"

But a stranger's voice, breathless, determined, drowned out the sound of his own strangled sob.

"You are too young to die, boy. Life is precious. Every day is a gift from God. I know how you feel. They have turned me back today, also, paying my passage as no doubt they have paid yours, but I would hate myself if I did not save you. Believe me, one day you will be glad."

A Dream of Aaron 〜

After Mama's going, Hannah could not find it in her heart to return to school, despite all of Papa's and Aunt Yehudis's pleading. Day after day, she played the violin. Night after night, she went to bed early, eager for the miracle that occurred as soon as she shut her eyes.

It was then that she saw Mama again in the house. This Mama was no longer sick and heartbroken; she was happy and beautiful. She always wore her Sabbath wig, her best black dress, and her pearls. She sang as she went about her work.

One night Mama was plucking a white goose half as big as a lion, so that the pillows she stuffed with its feathers nearly filled the kitchen. Another night she was sewing a beautiful silk wedding dress for Rachel, a dress with a queen's train so long that it flowed away out the door.

Sometimes it was the Sabbath, and the family was gathered about the supper table. Papa had brought home from *shul,* not one or two hungry guests, but a whole company, all of them pale, finely dressed *yeshiva* students with curling earlocks. Mama lit the Sabbath candles, one candle for each family member, and shielded her eyes as she murmured her prayers. The light of the fresh candle flames shone through her raised hands and made the flesh glow pink. At Papa's place, the Sabbath *hallah* was as exquisitely braided as if it had been carved.

Especially wonderful was the night Hannah dreamed of a Passover *seder*. Papa reclining upon a couchful of goose-down pillows . . . Mama so happy that her eyes shone like stars . . . the chairs filled with guests and family members, some of whom Hannah had never seen before but knew instantly, among them Great-aunt Soren with the bright red hair . . . on the table, the succession of holiday foods, the *matzo*, the bitter herbs, the boiled egg, all the rest . . . at each person's place, a wineglass, and before an empty place, one other glass for the Prophet Elijah, who might at any moment, seen or unseen, come walking in at the door.

A wineglass for Elijah?

Or for Aaron?

All at once, the scene shifted. Hannah was swept far away out of the *shtetl*. Out of the Passover springtime. To another season. To Aaron. By some magic which she did not question, she *became* Aaron . . . was one with a young soldier exchanging guard duty on the outer edge of a huge night encampment whose fires had long since burned to ash. The sky was moonless, the whole world so black that the young soldier could not see the face of the man who came to relieve him, could only feel the warmth of the body coming close to him in the dark.

As their shoulders touched, the unseen one's voice sounded, no louder than a whisper, yet as clear as though he had shouted.

"I have been thinking," the man said, "that I have never

known such a growing season as this on the steppes. I have
never known a wheat field as tall and thick as the one that lies
west of our camp. Lying in that wheat, a man would seem no
larger than a field mouse. Besides, our officers are not sharp-
eyed. And they are sleeping. It will be many hours before they
can follow us."

"Then, you mean—now?"

"Yes, now. You are young and strong. I am a veteran.
I know the countryside well."

"They will never find us!"

It was as if the young man's tense whisper were a pass-
word long agreed upon between them, a signal singing for
weeks in their blood. Upon toes as lightly placed as swallows'
feet, they began to move together, side by side, through the
darkness. Gradually, as the distance widened between them and
the post they had abandoned, they moved more quickly.

After what seemed an immeasurable length of time, they
began to run. A pale gold smudge upon the horizon grew
distinct, grew closer.

All at once, they reached it. The first tall wheat stalks
crackled about their churning legs. Again, as if at a signal, they
threw themselves down into the closely planted field. Gasping
for breath and shocked by the first sharp slash of the stalks at
his unprotected face, the young soldier longed to lie still to
recover, but the veteran's rough hand pulled him on.

"No stopping now."

On their bellies, half-smothered, they crawled forward,
though not so swiftly as to make the wheat whistle about
them. Ahead, the dim gold through which they moved ap-

peared to stretch endlessly. The whole world must be covered by this wheat field!

Abruptly, a sound as sharp as a musket shot shattered the silence. The sound became footsteps.

"They—they have seen us!"

"Still! Lie still!" the older man hissed.

So, locked in a fierce embrace, the two lay motionless. The heavy heads of the wheat, like some vast goose-down pillow, closed suffocatingly above them. Although the young soldier thought the pain in his chest would tear him apart, he managed to hold his breath.

Meanwhile, the footsteps approached, now sounding somehow like the beat of Papa's loom. They came near. If I should cough, the young soldier thought. . . . But the footsteps did not pause, only moved on steadily till they were lost in the night.

"It was no one. A peasant. An animal, even," the veteran rasped. "We must go on farther. We must go on until dawn."

So they continued, sometimes moving along upon bent knees like Russian dancers urged on by an unseen fiddler, sometimes crawling painfully on their stomachs deep in the never-ending wheat. The sky was just beginning to lighten when, by unspoken agreement, they decided to stand upright, breathe deep, and take the measure of their surroundings.

But as they rose no sight of fields or roads or houses met their view. Instead, they found themselves staring into the face of a peasant boy, his pale eyes blinking. Hannah had seen that face once before in the *shtetl,* been threatened by it. "If you come near, I will poke out your eyes," she had cried.

"I will poke out your eyes," the young soldier echoed, and the boy gave a strangled cry, backed away, and then turned and ran precipitously down a narrow path through the wheat.

"He saw our uniforms and thought we were soldiers. He may have hidden some treasure in this field, an amber necklace or a gold pin, and thought we would take it." The veteran's voice was grim. "Or he may have gone to report us. We must not wait for him to return."

So they sank back to their knees and crawled on, no longer daring to lift their heads above the stalks. Their chests heaved ever more cruelly with each drawn breath, until at last the morning sky was bright above them.

Swiftly, they made themselves a nest in the flowing grain, a nest also made up, curiously, of goose-down covers. The older soldier left just enough of an opening above their heads to allow them a ration of fresh air.

"Only if someone stumbles upon us will they see us lying here," he said. "We must rest till evening. Then we must travel on. Somewhere, we will rid ourselves of these uniforms, find other clothes. All that will come in time."

As they rested, the young soldier suddenly stared at the dirt-caked back turned toward him, the bent, grizzled head.

"It is so—so strange," he whispered. "We do not know each other's names, and I am sure I would not have recognized you if you had approached me in the light. Even now, I have not truly seen your face."

"You may not know me, boy," the rough voice answered. "I have watched *you* since the day you arrived in the regiment. In that miserable camp, you held yourself apart. Like a prince. You were strong and desperate. That is the best combination for an escape—if an older head is also there. An older head remembers much. Remembers, the principal thing, bread and water. Here—eat, drink."

"You are very kind," the young soldier murmured, feeling the crust of hard bread thrust into his fist. "It is true I am so hungry I could faint. But do you know that to live I must have not only bread? I must also have my violin."

There was no answer, for all at once Hannah woke up, trembling violently as though the earth itself had quaked beneath her bed. For the first instant, she scarcely knew whether her soul was in her own body or in Aaron's. Then she saw the smudgy gray line of the bed curtains, felt the goose-down covers that had fallen, twisted, to her side.

She lay without sleeping for the rest of the night.

Leah ☙

Soon after the dream of Aaron, Hannah found the daytime *shtetl* world of sunshine and solid flesh as startling as the world of night. Her bewilderment was sharpened one spring morning, many months following Mama's death, when Papa poured fingernail water over his hands as usual, said his prayers, and ate the breakfast that she had prepared for him. Then, flushing as rosy as an embarrassed boy, he announced that he would be inviting a visitor to the house. No, not a *yeshiva* student. Nor a needy traveler. It would be a young woman. Leah was her name.

"You will like her. She is a good person," Papa said.

Yet he delayed bringing the guest home for four days, five, six. When he brought her at last, after a week's time, he was scarcely able to speak more words than the names stammered for an introduction. In an uneasy silence, the three of them, Papa, Hannah, and Leah, sat down for tea beside the kitchen stove.

Hannah made her tea syrupy with extra jam, since Papa seemed not to notice the extravagance. That was, in itself, a test. Leah, for her part, spooned only a few cautious droplets into her glass. She looked from one to the other of them as

99

if frightened to have taken even that much. Indeed, Hannah thought, Leah looked frightened altogether. Her hands, with their broken fingernails, shook as she clutched her glass.

As Papa had said, she was a young woman. But Papa had *not* said that she was sallow-skinned, with dark circles under her hazel eyes. Nor that she was thin and awkward, and moved as if she were afraid she might break something, even herself. Her fear proved to be justified. After sipping cautiously at her glass for little more than a moment, she nearly spilled a surge of the hot liquid into her lap. As she daubed miserably at the splatter of drops that darkened her skirt, Papa cleared his throat.

Papa spoke loudly. Though such a gentle man, he often spoke loudly, Hannah had noticed, when he was frightened or deeply moved.

"You and Leah must come to know each other well, *maidele*," he declared.

"How are we to do that, Papa? Is Leah to come to tea again?" Hannah raised her eyes to see his face as flushed as it had been the week before. He fell silent.

Only that night, as the two of them, father and daughter, sat alone at the supper table, was his courage renewed.

"You must understand, *maidele*," he murmured. "Leah has agreed to become my wife."

"Your—your *wife*?"

The next morning, Hannah rushed away to Aunt Yehudis, filled with fury and distress.

"Papa has forgotten Mama!" she cried in Aunt Yehudis's

tiny earthen-floored kitchen with its faltering fire. "Why should he take a new wife?"

"A man needs a live woman, not a beautiful memory, at his side," Aunt Yehudis replied slowly.

"I do not see why!"

"To take care of him, of course."

"But *I* take care of him! I promised Mama that I would. Does he think I mean to break my promise?"

Aunt Yehudis shook her head as if to a stupid one.

"You are only nine, *liebchen*."

"I am going to be ten!" Hannah insisted. "I watched Mama and Rachel. I can keep the house. I know how to do it all."

"You may know how, but you have not the time, Hannah. You must go back to school soon. Reb Doddl is waiting for you. You must become a learned woman." Suddenly, tears sprang into Aunt Yehudis's eyes. "I would not say this to every girl. I did not say this even to your mother. But it is my greatest sorrow that I can scarcely do more than read the women's prayers and scribble a poor letter—that I am an ignoramus. A stupid old woman."

"You are not old! You are not stupid!" Hannah objected.

"Of that you are a poor judge." Aunt Yehudis sternly wiped her eyes. "I am as I say I am, and you are not to grow up like me. For my sake, you must learn to use your head."

"But it is not a matter of my head," Hannah cried helplessly. "Papa has forgotten Mama. How could he? Mama was so beautiful, so clever. While Leah—Leah—" The name choked off all other words in her throat.

Gently, Aunt Yehudis took her hand.

"There are different kinds of love, *maidele*. I myself have known more than one kind. Your papa will never forget your mama, so beautiful, so accomplished. Leah is different, so solemn, so frightened. He will protect her. It will be a *mitzvah*, a blessing, to him just to see her smile. In her own way, Leah also will make your Papa happy."

"No one else would have her! That much is certain." Hannah gave one last, desperate scowl.

"You are right, *maidele,*" Aunt Yehudis said with a nod. "If your papa had not chosen Leah, she would be a leftover, doomed to be alone in the world all the days of her life."

In spite of her despair, Hannah was thunderstruck.

"Alone in the world?"

"Did your papa not tell you? Leah is an orphan. Her family was killed in a *pogram* long ago. She does not remember how she herself escaped the marauders, only that as a little girl she wandered from place to place with strangers who at last left her here in the *shtetl*. She does not even know her mama's and papa's names."

A chill shook Hannah. Not to have a family, not to remember Mama and Papa and Aaron and the others. Horrified, she stood mute as Aunt Yehudis spoke again. "You must show respect to your papa's new wife. The *shtetl* is buying a wedding dress and brandy. It will be a simple celebration, since it is your papa's second marriage and the bride is so poor. Yet they must go beneath the canopy and be blessed."

Aunt Yehudis repeated, this time sternly, since Hannah herself had not yet found words. "Though she is a poor orphan, Hannah, you must show respect to your papa's new wife."

Despite Hannah's first resolve to obey Aunt Yehudis, during that summer after the wedding nothing went well in the house. Sometimes, at night, Hannah peeked out between her bed curtains and listened to Leah breathing peacefully upon Mama's pillow. Then she would draw back under her covers and fight back sobs.

In the daytime, things were worse. Leah began to grow plumper and more confident. She began to hum at her work, but she had no more voice than a bullfrog. Hannah herself played the violin in the farthest corner of the loft so that she would not have to hear that hoarse, tuneless sound.

Leah was little better at housework. Although it was true that she was forever sweeping and scrubbing and that the kitchen shone like glass every day of the week, she had no other talent. The farmers often cheated her at the market, so that the money Mama and Rachel had once stretched to feed eight scarcely fed three so well. Leah was a poor cook, too. The soup was always half-wasted, boiling down to a thick, scorched broth or foaming and spilling over the sides of the pot. The bread came out of the oven gummy from undercooking or so hard that Hannah feared she would break a tooth trying to eat it. As for sewing, the patches Leah stitched on Papa's trousers soon worked loose and flapped about his thin legs like a flight of moths. Hannah was ashamed to see him when he walked in the street.

Aunt Yehudis made excuses.

"I have told you that Leah is an orphan. She had no one to teach her when she was growing up. She had not your clever Mama or Rachel. But she tries hard to get things right."

"She does *not* get them right! She does not learn. Not even when I show her."

"Give her time, *maidele.* Give her time."

As the months passed, Hannah asked herself indignantly, how much time. She had by now returned to her lessons with Reb Doddl, but her worried thoughts remained at home. She despaired not only for herself—for Papa's sake, she felt doubly ashamed. He deserved a wife who was skillful and clever, one who would not disgrace him.

It was on an unforgettable Sabbath that Papa took a great risk. He announced that he would bring a guest home to supper from *shul,* the first Sabbath guest since his wedding.

"The rabbi has asked me to do this," he explained to a trembling Leah. "He has asked me also to let the man sleep in our house. He knows that we have room. This will not be hard for us, Leah. It will be a *mitzvah* to us. You must not be anxious."

In the old days, Hannah remembered, Papa had often brought home visitors. Penniless students who ate at different tables in the *shtetl* every week. Strangers away from home on long journeys. Sometimes even a holy man or a traveling scholar. The rabbi had always known that, though the Eliashovs were poor, Papa's conversation was learned and Mama could make a feast from noodles alone.

Papa had loved all these visitors and the long hours with

them. As they had talked, his mild weekday face had been transformed.

Despite Papa's encouragement to Leah, his face betrayed his anxiety when, with the dusk long since deepened, he brought the stranger in at the kitchen door.

"*A gutn Shabbas.* Good Sabbath. This is Reb Abba, Leah. God be praised, he comes to share the Sabbath meal with us."

At those words, Leah, taking a long, earnest look at the newcomer, took a deep breath and retreated to her stove. Hannah herself lingered uneasily in the kitchen shadows until they had all been summoned to the supper table. There, in the candlelight, she inspected their guest.

Reb Abba, she saw, was a shabbily dressed man, not young, not old. He had a bald head and a few lank brown hairs for earlocks, a jagged scar across one rough, deeply tanned cheek, and eyes that were oddly burning. Surely he was not a student. Not with those stumpy, only half-clean hands. Nor was he a traveler bent upon business. Nor a holy man, nor a scholar. Mystery hung about him like an invisible cloak. Scarcely realizing how intensely she was staring until his eyes abruptly turned away from her, Hannah watched his gaze sweep around the table until it came to rest upon Leah.

Alas, as one could have guessed, Leah was failing them! No wonder the stranger stared. The Sabbath wig, which always made her, unlike Mama, look like a little girl playing grown-up, sat askew above her thin face. Her cheeks, in the dim light, showed an absurd riot of color, now a rush of pink, now deathly white. The *hallah,* which she had forgotten earlier and now carried late to the table, was coarsely braided, a lump. She laid the knife on the plate beside it carelessly, and so when Papa reached to cut the loaf, the shining blade fell to the floor.

A terrible silence! Papa and Leah stared down, round-eyed, at the knife on the floor, not knowing, Hannah saw, which of them should pick it up. Would it be a reproof to Leah if Papa retrieved it? But what if Leah bent, or both of them together, bumping their heads?

Something must be said, something done to divert the visitor's attention. Into the silence, Hannah spoke with a firm, determined voice.

"You are a stranger, Reb Abba. Have you come to stay in the *shtetl*?"

The visitor gingerly shook his head.

"Are you going on a journey, then?"

To Hannah's surprise, Reb Abba darted her a frightened look and then turned anxiously toward Papa. His Adam's apple leaped in his pipe-thin throat. Had he swallowed a walnut? Was that why he would not speak?

"Are you going on a *long* journey?" she persisted, her curiosity aroused.

As if in spite of himself, the man made an uncertain motion with his mouth.

"Y-yes . . . a long journey . . . I believe, y-yes."

"To Bialystok? To Warsaw?" And, as she saw him continue to look doubtful, his glance sliding from Papa to Leah and back, "To America?"

Then, all at once, though Hannah herself had not known that the words were coming, and though she was not sure that she had ever clearly thought them before, she made a breathless announcement.

"I can tell you, Reb Abba, that I myself mean to go to America."

"You!" Leah gasped. She reached for the fallen knife and clattered it down beside the *hallah,* but Hannah went on swiftly.

"Yes. Someday I am going to America. I am going to find Chaim and Rachel and Muni. I am going to find my brother Aaron. He will teach me more about the violin. One day, in America, I will be a musician."

"Zavel, Zavel! Stop the child!" It was Leah's voice, thin with shock.

Strangely, the visitor appeared even more distressed than Leah. He seemed almost to bounce in his chair as Hannah continued.

"You see, Reb Abba, my brother Chaim and my sister Rachel—Moishe Kopsofsky's Rachel—are already in America. In Youngstown, Ohio, and in Pittsburgh, Pennsylvania. About Muni, we don't know for sure. He ran away in the night. The soldiers of the Tsar's army took my brother Aaron, but someday Aaron will escape and find us." Then, suddenly, something in the man's burning eyes gave Hannah a chill. "You do think, Reb Abba, that Aaron can escape from the Tsar's army? It happens, so Papa and Aunt Yehudis say. You are a traveler, going a long way, meeting many people. You should know."

Disaster! With a shudder, Reb Abba sank his face into his hands.

"Zavel, stop the child's chattering!" Leah cried.

At the end of the table, Papa's gentle face turned crimson, his mild eyes flashed. He gave Hannah a terrible glance.

Silenced, she, too, bent her face into her hands.

As for the visitor, he now seemed to find himself unable to begin his supper. At Papa's grave invitation, he shambled away up the loft stairs. As he vanished into the darkness, the low candle sputtering in his hand, Leah began to weep miserably.

"You must punish the child, Zavel. Such a shame to you! A child, a girl, to ask such questions of the Sabbath guest! To upset him so badly! And to say such wild things, such foolishness! To tell lies!"

Papa took his wife's arm.

"Wipe your eyes and go to bed, Leah," he directed gently. "You can straighten the table later. None of us is hungry now. And I *will* talk with Hannah."

He did so when the two of them were left alone.

"You did not behave well, *maidele*. Leah is right about that. A young girl should keep silent before strangers—though, in truth, silence has never been your gift. This I will tell you now, and you must promise never to repeat a word of what I say. *Reb Abba may be in great danger.* Who he is, or even if Reb Abba is his real name, no one in the *shtetl* knows."

At that moment, her ears already pounding with excitement, Hannah heard a sound even more astonishing than Papa's words. Down the loft stairs came the hoarsely whistled notes of a melody Papa could never recognize but which rang in her head, unmistakable.

The melody was the mazurka. *Chopin's mazurka—and Aaron's!*

The next morning, her composure returned, Leah climbed the loft stairs. "I must tell our visitor that it is time for breakfast and *shul*. I have not heard him stir."

Soon she returned to the kitchen, stumbling in great haste, her face dead white.

"Zavel!" she cried. "Zavel, the stranger has already gone away. I think he did not even sleep in the bed. The covers are so smooth. And, Zavel, *he has stolen Aaron's violin!*"

Papa sprang up from the table as though jerked by some powerful, unseen hand.

"Stolen Aaron's violin?" he echoed. "Oh, no, Leah! No! That can't be!"

But it was so, despite Papa's stunned disbelief. Although the three of them searched the loft, every cranny of it, they found no trace of the precious instrument. Only as they dropped numbly into their chairs beside the kitchen table did Hannah at last dare to speak.

"I—I think that Reb Abba has taken the violin to Aaron, Papa. I think that Aaron sent him to get it—and to bring us a sign that he is safe."

Leah's eyes flew open wide. She put her hand over her lips.

"Oh, no, I—Zavel, must we listen to the child again?"

Papa turned his head solemnly.

"Why do you say such a mad thing, *maidele?*" he demanded.

"It is not mad. Aaron would not have dared to return to us here, but he *did* send us a sign."

"A sign?"

"Yes. The melody of the mazurka. I heard Reb Abba whistling it from the loft. Chopin's mazurka, which Aaron arranged!"

"I—I did not hear it—" But Papa faltered, flushing. When had he ever claimed a musical ear?

Finally Leah stormed through her tears.

"Such wild talk! Who can believe it? I tell you, Zavel, Reb Abba was no escaped soldier. I am certain of it. *He was my papa.* I knew it the moment he came into the house."

This time Papa's face became yet more solemn, more astounded.

"Leah, Leah! I cannot believe that you are saying such a thing. You must always have longed to find your people, but longing is not knowing. After so many years, you could not hope to remember your papa."

"That is true." Leah nodded jerkily, stifling a fresh sob. "It has been as though I had never had a papa. Yet, last night, when I looked at Reb Abba, something turned in my head. Even if that had not happened, there was the way *he* looked at *me*. He could not keep his eyes from me. Surely you saw that, Zavel."

"Yes, I saw. Like all lonely men, poor travelers who go from town to town, our visitor was not used to seeing a woman in her own home—a woman—" Papa's voice took on a soft pride—"who is to have a child. It was for such reasons that he stared at you, Leah. He wanted to feast his eyes."

"Do you think that truly, Zavel? Do you think I deceived myself?"

"Yes, I think that. Reb Abba could not have been your papa. My Leah's papa would never have been a thief."

Yet Reb Abba could have been Aaron's friend, his rescuer. And no thief.

In the trembling silence at the table, Hannah dared not say that thought aloud. Nor did she dare repeat Papa's startling words, "a woman who is to have a child."

Leah, then, was to have a baby!

The Twins ✍

Five months later, on a fine spring day when warm breezes blew through the *shtetl,* Papa met Hannah at the kitchen door as she returned from a day at the market with Aunt Yehudis. His eyes were shining with a happiness Hannah had not seen there since Aaron had been taken away.

"Great news, *maidele*!" he cried. "You have a new sister. More than that." He paused dramatically. "You have *two* new sisters."

"Two new sisters?" Hannah demanded.

Papa nodded energetically. It was as though he was a young man. "God be praised, there are once again twins in my house."

When Papa took Hannah into the bedroom, the little ones were laid out on pillows beside their mother. Each was wrapped in long strips of cotton and had a tiny cap pulled down over her small head. Only the half-closed eyes, so red-lidded, and the wee button noses that showed between the enveloping folds of white cloth, proved that there were babies inside.

"They are beautiful," declared the stout neighbor woman who was bustling around the crowded bed. "Already they're so heavy one can't lift them."

They looked no heavier than feather balls, Hannah thought. As for beautiful—

In spite of herself, Hannah's gaze next fell upon Leah. She was glowing with a light that seemed to shine through her. She smiled up at Papa weakly but joyously.

"Next year I will give you a son, Zavel," she whispered.

"That will be as God wills it." Tenderly Papa bent over the bed. "This year I am more than content. You have given me two fine daughters, and you yourself are well. It is a blessing."

"You are so good to me, Zavel." Leah gave a deep, satisfied sigh then turned toward the babies on their pillows.

As she looked from one small daughter to the other, reaching out a wondering finger to touch each tiny nose, a further change came over her such as Hannah could not have imagined. Her smile, which had glowed shyly up at Papa, was all unabashed radiance now. She was beautiful.

Leah was beautiful.

For the first time, Leah has someone who belongs to her, Hannah thought. She no longer feels like an orphan. But *I*— she stared at the four of them, Papa, Leah, and the babies in their tight, adoring circle—*I* truly am an orphan now!

A hammer of despair beat inside her chest. She crept out of the bedroom. No one followed or called after her. For a long moment she stood, alone and motionless, in the kitchen corner beside Papa's loom.

Still no one noticed that she had left the room. No one came to her.

Abruptly she reached for the pen, ink, and paper on the shelf beside the loom. With these Papa kept his accounts, but he would not miss them today. Hands cupped about her newly seized plunder, she hurried breathlessly toward the loft. Up the steep steps she scrambled, the hammer pounding ever more fiercely in her chest.

At the top of the stairs, she paused to look about her.

No one had come into the loft since the morning after Reb Abba's departure. During the frosty winter, no one had wanted to bear the cold there. Today dust motes rose into the beam of pale light from the small, unwashed window. The spring breeze outside had had no chance to freshen the stale air. Underfoot the floorboards squealed as Hannah stepped impulsively across them.

No matter! She sat down upon the splintery floor and began a letter. She must think of nothing else. There must be no mistakes, no misunderstandings. These were the most important words she had ever written in her life.

In the weeks and months that followed, Hannah grew more and more convinced that she had been right to send the letter. Not only did she no longer have the comfort of her music, but also there seemed to be no place for her in the house.

The twins were tiny, but the house was full of them. From all over the *shtetl,* people came bustling and clucking to see the two babies, so beautiful and just alike. Neighbors brought pots of rich soup and meat for Leah so that she would be strong enough to nurse both of her children. Leah herself continued to glow with pride.

As for Papa, he worked contentedly hour after hour at his loom. Though a shy man, Papa had always been delighted to have his house full of music, chatter, and life. Since the loss of Aaron, the departure of the younger brothers, and then the loss of Mama, Hannah decided that the silence of the house must have weighed far more heavily upon him than she had guessed. Now, though he talked no more than usual, he smiled a proud welcome to every visitor. He even neglected his beloved studies. With two new daughters and a son promised for next year, he wove industriously, importantly, clackety-clack.

All that summer, Hannah waited, her secret burning inside her. She scarcely knew herself, she had become so silent. And despite the general preoccupation with the babies, the family began to notice her change.

"Bortsch and bread make a girl's cheeks red," Aunt Yehudis declared, offering her food. Then, more sternly, "You shut yourself away from us, *maidele*. You are a nutshell that will not be pried open."

"Hannah has become a stranger," Papa said with a sigh.

"She does not love the babies," Leah declared.

Everything they said was true except the last. Hannah had begun to admit to herself that little Mashka and Eidel were fine babies, and they grew more lovely with each passing day.

Though she pretended at first not to be watching them, she always managed to be near when Leah took off their thick cotton wrappings and let them squirm freely on the bed. Such strong pink legs and arms, always moving and stretching. Such flawless hands and feet, each tiny finger and toe so perfect. Even the awkward button noses were beginning to take a delicate shape. It was a special, though secret, pride to Hannah that only she and their mother could tell the two little girls apart.

One day, when a neighbor called Leah into the kitchen, Hannah quickly stepped to the bedside for fear the babies would roll off onto the floor. As she bent above them, Eidel caught at a strand of her bright red hair. Mashka smiled at her, a wobbly smile all twinkling blue eyes and flower mouth.

"I love you!" Hannah whispered in a rush of adoration and hugged them both, though Eidel still tugged painfully at her hair.

After that day, she hugged the little ones often when no one else was near, and she forgot to frown when Leah asked her to watch over them. Her happiest moments of the long summer were spent at their side.

Yet she must not lose her resolve. The more beautiful the babies grew, the more surely she knew that Papa no longer needed her, that she had no place here. She had been right to send her letter. If only the answer were not so long in coming!

It was on a cold September day, when frost lay thick on the spindly leaves in the garden, that Hannah's waiting ended. Two envelopes, both addressed in Rachel's awkward hand, arrived at the door. One of the envelopes was addressed to Papa, and the other, to Hannah herself.

Hannah seized hers and ran into the bedroom to tear it open. To her fury, she was blinded by hot tears. When at last she had wiped her eyes dry and could make out the words, she was interrupted by Papa's anxious call from the kitchen.

As she approached him, he sat before his loom, his beard not quite hiding his trembling lips. Sadly, he nodded toward the letter in his lap.

"You never told us, *maidele,*" he murmured. "You never said that you were writing to Rachel."

"That's true. It is—it is also true that I used your pen and paper, Papa, though I spent my own coins—I had saved them —to pay for the stamp."

Papa shook his head vaguely. It was as though he had not heard her last words, as though they were of no account. From the far side of the kitchen, Leah quickly came to stand at his side, her hand tightening upon his shoulder. He shifted in his chair.

"Then I must believe what Rachel writes here. You want to leave us, Hannah. You want to go to America."

"Yes."

"But why? Such a young girl!"

"Do you not see? I am an orphan here, without Mama."

At that Papa's eyes flooded with tears. A man, crying!

"I—I still cannot believe this, *maidele.* I had hoped that you and Leah could come to understand and love each other. *Both* of you are orphans. It should have been easy to find the way to each other's hearts. I know that she wanted it to happen."

Hannah lifted her chin stubbornly.

"Leah has the twins, Papa. She does not need me."

"Even if that were true, *I* need you."

"No, not now. You have Leah and Eidel and Mashka to keep you happy." Then, as Papa rubbed at his streaming eyes and Leah herself remained stiffly at his side, a new fear stabbed at Hannah.

"You *will* say yes, Papa? You won't say that I can't go to America? Oh, Papa, you must not say no!"

"How shall I say yes or no so quickly?" Papa stammered. "I—I m-must have t-time to think. Such a problem. You are such a little girl, Hannah. Only nine years old."

"I am ten now," cried Hannah. "I have been ten for three months. You do not even remember my age. Rachel writes me that I must have your permission to go, but you cannot say no. You *must* not. If you do, I—I will run away like Muni!"

Leah paled, shocked.

"Zavel, the child must not speak so to her papa!"

But Hannah rushed desperately to the door and hurried away into the street, leaving the two of them standing open-mouthed behind her. Through the windy *shtetl,* with dry autumn leaves flying about her, she ran. To Aunt Yehudis's and Uncle Nahum's gray, tumbledown house.

Breathless and chilled, she flung open the door and plunged into her aunt's tiny kitchen. She had come away from home so impulsively that she had not so much as snatched up a scarf.

"You are shaking, Hannah!" cried Aunt Yehudis, springing up from her chair, knitting needles flying. "You look so strange. God forbid, some terrible thing has happened? To your papa and Leah? To the twins?"

Even Uncle Nahum threw down his newspaper to stare at her, though when he tried to speak he coughed.

"Papa and Leah and the twins are well," she gasped. "I will tell you everything as soon as I can."

When she had got her breath and, at Aunt Yehudis's insistence, warmed herself with a glass of hot tea, she read aloud Rachel's letter.

Dear Little Sister,
You ask me how my life is in America. Let me tell you. As Mama dreamed, my Moishe and I are free and happy here. We have already one son, Leibel. He is shy and gentle like our lost brother. Another little one is to be born soon. All of us are well.

It is true what we were told in the *shtetl.* Here no *pograms* sweep away Jewish lives and fortunes. No soldiers come to drag young men off to the army. But it is also true that in America we have seen no streets paved with gold. People struggle. My Moishe works from dawn till dusk and is far from rich. We have an apartment with three small rooms.

You ask another thing. Would we give you a home with us here? Oh, *liebchen,* it is my dearest wish that someday all of the Eliashovs can come to America. You yourself will be welcome at any time. I never cease being lonely for you.

But it is Papa who must decide this question. I cannot ask him to send me his ten-year-old daughter if he cannot find the wish in his own heart. I am writing to him.

Your Rachel

When Hannah had finished the letter, there was silence in the drafty kitchen except for the sputter of a coal in the wheezing fire in the stove, and for Uncle Nahum's cough as he rose and hobbled on his crutches to the bedroom.

Aunt Yehudis spoke at last.

"Even I am astonished that you have made such a request, *maidele.* But one thing is certain. You cannot go alone to

America. *That,* your papa will never allow. There are great dangers."

"You yourself have said that I could find my way to China," Hannah protested hotly.

"This is not the same. You forget that our Leibel was crushed beneath cartwheels, that Muni has vanished altogether. For a girl there are perils I cannot name."

"Why, then, you must come with me!"

"*I?*"

"Yes." Hannah's pulse throbbed wildly. "We must go together, Aunt Yehudis. Why have we not thought of it before? You, too, dream. You want a house where the shingles do not sigh on the roof when the wind is strong, where there is always enough wood for the fire. I am sure of it!"

"You are wrong, *maidele.*" Aunt Yehudis shook her head. "Oh, it is true that in my girlhood I had my own visions, not of great houses and far countries but of learning. I longed to read books like a man. I fell in love with a rich young rabbi's son who promised to teach me, but when the *pogrom* made our family penniless, my fiancé broke our engagement. Papa could no longer give me a dowry. Perhaps your mama never had the heart to tell you that old story. Nor the story of your papa, a poor scholar whom my parents were proud to accept as a son-in-law because he was so learned. When they could no longer support him at his studies, Zavel was obliged to become a water carrier, then a drayman and then, at last, a weaver." Once again Aunt Yehudis shook her head. "Alas, *maidele,* your papa's and my young dreams died long ago."

"Dreams don't die, Aunt Yehudis," Hannah declared. "I relive mine every day."

"With me, things are different, child. It is true that when good luck comes knocking at the door, a wise woman says, 'Quick! Come take a chair.' But good luck has not knocked at my door for many years. I no longer expect it."

"You could earn enough money to go to America, Aunt Yehudis. You are so clever at sewing and knitting. You could soon earn enough for the steamship ticket and the money needed at Ellis Island."

"If I worked hard and gave up everything in my house, I could never earn so much."

"In America, you will earn even more. Come with me and send back the steamship ticket for Uncle Nahum."

One last time, Aunt Yehudis shook her head.

"They will never let Nahum come in at Ellis Island. It is not a matter of money only. America does not want a man whose brains burn in his head, who reads every line of print that comes his way, but who has only a poor, twisted body and a cough that goes on night and day.

"If my Nahum came to Ellis Island with ten gold rings on his fingers, they would still turn him back. You must see for yourself now, *maidele.* I have chosen my own life, and I am not sorry for it. But I cannot go to America. I can never take you there."

The Journey ✒

Hannah did not lose heart.

That night she saw Mama again in her dreams. She was at a distance, upon a curving, unknown road. Her body seemed to be floating mistily inside the billowing sweep of a cloudlike skirt. Her face was once more young and happy, her hair floating about it. She was singing with that lovely voice Hannah had once known so well.

All at once, a violin appeared in her arms. She lifted the bow to the strings, played an accompaniment to her song, and then nodded and extended a beckoning finger toward her daughter.

"You must come to America, Hannah," she called and, smiling, beckoning still, vanished down the mysterious road.

It was a sign! Hannah knew that, even as she wakened. Papa would grant her his permission soon. He could not resist the will of Mama in heaven, Mama with a violin.

In fact, it was the very next day that Aunt Yehudis appeared in the kitchen doorway. In her hand, she held a tarnished silver brooch.

"This brooch once belonged to Great-aunt Soren, from whom our Hannah has got her red hair," she announced to

Papa. "It is worn thin and the clasp is bent, but I shall straighten and polish it. I will take it to the market next week. Some peasant boy will buy it as a gift for his sweetheart. That money will help send Hannah to America."

"Help send Hannah to America! But I have not said—"

Aunt Yehudis did not wait for Papa's words. She went on briskly. "I have never loved jewelry. I have not so much as looked at this brooch for years. I found it only this morning at the back of a cupboard, like a crumb from last year's bread.

"The important thing is, Zavel," she said as she faced Papa boldly, "that Hannah must have her chance. There is no future for her here in the *shtetl,* where our young people grow poorer day by day. Her sister offers her a home in America. God willing, she will find her fortune there. You cannot refuse her request."

Slowly, so slowly that Hannah thought she would faint from holding her breath, Papa nodded.

"You are right, Yehudis. I did not sleep last night as I thought of all these things. I shall miss my daughter, but I cannot hold her back."

With a cry, Hannah rushed to his side.

"Thank you, Papa. Oh, thank you!"

Gently he took her hand.

"There remains the matter of a fit companion and of more money, child. The sale of the silver brooch will not add up to the rest of the sum needed to send you to America. We cannot find more *zlotys* overnight."

Indeed, collecting the sum needed was hard.

Rachel, in her letter to Papa, had promised to pay for half

of this steamship ticket. "Forgive me. It is all I can send just now. With our little Leibel, and a baby on the way, Moishe and I have no more extra money. We dare not borrow. And Chaim no longer writes to us at all. We do not know why."

Mama's treasure box had, of course, long been emptied.

"And, alas, out of snow you can't make cheesecake," Aunt Yehudis declared wryly.

Hannah heard Leah and Papa gravely discussing the matter one night.

"There are goose-down covers on Hannah's bed," Papa murmured behind the bed curtains. "The twins will not need them for a while, and they will bring a good price."

But Hannah heard Leah give a little sob.

"Is it so hard to part with the covers?" Papa asked softly.

"No, it is not that. It is the memories. I can never forget the terrible times, Zavel. When I was a little girl and the soldiers came, they poked their bayonets into all our goose-down covers. The feathers flew like snow in the house. I cannot remember my mama and papa, but I remember the flying feathers. Forgive me."

Papa soothed Leah with little clucks as though she were an injured child, then Hannah heard him go on with his plans.

"There is more news which I have not yet told you, Leah. The rabbi stopped me today in the street. His grandson must have a *talis,* a prayer shawl, and there is not time to send away to a weaver in Bialystok. The rabbi will place his order with me. He will pay me well. We could spare some of that money for Hannah. Are you willing?"

"I am willing. Yes, of course."

"God be praised, you are a good woman, Leah. Thank you."

So, in a dozen ways, the money was gathered, but there was still the problem of the companion.

When Hannah lay in bed thinking of the train she must board, the trip to Warsaw, the journey across Poland and Germany to Antwerp, the steamship and the crossing of the broad Atlantic Ocean, she was thrilled not with fear but with excitement. She would come to know those great, mysterious distances. She would see all the wonders Rachel and her brothers had seen. But Papa remained cautious, afraid. She must not go alone.

The first possible companion turned out to be Gitl, the butcher's daughter. Gitl's fiancé had gone to America, promising to send for her as soon as he could earn money for the passage. The money had never arrived. Aunt Yehudis heard a report that the fiancé, a lively young man from another *shtetl,* was courting a prosperous merchant's daughter in New York. Gitl had wailed and moped for months, demanding that her Papa himself pay for her passage. Wearied by his daughter's constant pleading and frightened by her pale face—"though one would swear she rubs flour into those cheeks," the butcher's neighbors murmured sagely—the poor father finally agreed to send Gitl on her way.

"But the girl is not fit company. She is a featherhead," Aunt Yehudis asserted.

"Gitl has always been a problem to her family," Papa acknowledged uneasily.

"She storms and stamps her feet. She is spoiled," Aunt Yehudis persisted. "Stupid."

"And so pretty," Leah said with a sigh. "Her lashes lie on her cheeks like black lace."

"Small comfort in that!" Aunt Yehudis retorted. "Aboard ship, the young men will flirt with her. She may forget her fiancé altogether. Worse yet, she may forget to watch over Hannah. And we all know that the world is a wicked place."

So in midwinter pretty Gitl boarded the train for Warsaw, her trunk heavy with linens and a pair of fine brass candlesticks, her suitcase stuffed with new clothes. But Hannah did not go with her.

The next person to leave for America was Reb Itzak's Aaron. Aunt Yehudis learned the details of this departure, too.

"Reb Itzak is in despair that his son is turning his back on the fur business, that he himself is to be left behind in the *shtetl* with only his poor, sickly wife. Aaron does not care. He is like Gitl, used to having his own way. He boasts that in America he will become far richer than his father."

Hannah remembered once again the terrible day when the soldiers had carried away the Eliashovs' Aaron, and the bribe that had been paid. "One thing is certain. I will not go to America with Reb Itzak's Aaron," she announced.

"No, not with that one," Aunt Yehudis seconded her fiercely. "May he lose all his teeth except one, and that one ache! In this cold, stormy weather, may he own five ships of gold and all of them sink!"

So the fur merchant's son, no doubt unaware of Aunt Yehudis's curse upon him, went away, and once again Hannah stayed behind.

"But I will not wait forever," she told herself resolutely. "I will find a companion for myself."

Two weeks later, on her way to market, she paused before the blacksmith's shop. Although she had always marveled at the beauty of the gold and crimson sparks that flew from the busy forge, today she found herself staring at a different sight. Sara, the blacksmith's frail eldest daughter, was waving a sheet of paper and struggling to make herself heard above the clangor. The smith was too engrossed in his heavy work to pause for her, and her timid voice was lost.

A moment later, apparently despairing of her efforts, the young woman pulled her heavy cape about her and came rushing out of the shop, still waving the paper. She was nearsighted, this Sara, and did not recognize Hannah until the two of them were scarcely more than an arm's length apart. Then her pale face lit up with excitement and relief.

"Hannah Eliashov, you have been to school. You must read this for me. It is a letter."

"A letter?"

"Yes, it must be—oh, I am certain it is from America, from Jacob, my husband, who went over the sea two years ago. In this time he has been ill, out of work, and so lonely for me and our baby, whom he has never seen, that he thought he would die. I thought I would die, also. But now—now—I beg you, tell me what he says!" Sara choked and lifted the folds of her thick cape to her eyes.

Hannah read the letter swiftly.

"Your Jacob will send you a steamship ticket, Sara." Her own voice was breathless. "He has enough money to bring you to America at last."

"And just when I had lost all hope that we would ever again be together!" Sara sobbed joyously. "Is it not a miracle, Hannah?"

"Yes, it is a miracle." Hannah nodded with a sudden, bursting enthusiasm of her own. "You must go to America as Jacob tells you, and I—I will go with you!"

In the Eliashov kitchen there was, of course, much hesitation about Hannah's swiftly taken decision.

"I must discuss this with the blacksmith," Papa fretted.

"How will Sara take care of Hannah when she has her own baby to tend?" Leah asked.

"I do not need to be taken care of!" Hannah cried. "I can take care of myself. Oh, Papa, you have promised! You cannot refuse me now."

Once again, Aunt Yehudis brought the argument to an end.

"Sara's baby—God bless him—he's only a year and a half old, and not strong. She will need help caring for that little one. Help, also, with all the directions, the strange places, the queer tongues. She is a good woman, pious and honest, but she has never learned more than her prayers. She will be lucky to have with her a clever girl like Hannah who speaks not only Yiddish but Polish, Russian, and some German, and who can read and write. You must arrange this at once with her father, Zavel."

"You are right as always, Yehudis. I will do as you say."
And Papa bowed his head.

It was not until the day of the departure, a fine spring morning
with all hint of frost gone from the air, that Hannah's courage
faltered ever so little. The family had come to the railroad
station to see her off. All of them were there—Aunt Yehudis,
Uncle Nahum, leaning upon his crutches, Papa, Leah, and the
twins, lately turned one year old.

She hugged the babies first and longest. Eidel twisted a
strand of her hair about one small fist. Mashka smiled. The two
little sisters, always lovely, had never looked so entirely beautiful to Hannah. She released them reluctantly to their mother
and then threw her arms around Papa.

"You must all come to America someday, Papa," she
begged.

"Who can foretell the future, *maidele*? God has sent
greater miracles."

But, even as he let her go, Hannah knew that Papa was
not a man for adventures. He loved his *shtetl,* his home, by
now even his loom. He loved the memories here, and he loved
his new wife.

As for Leah herself, she had already wandered too far in
her life. To have her own snug kitchen, her tiny garden, her
kind husband, her babies—all that was to be more than mistress
of a castle. Leah would never dare to cross the wide, mysterious ocean. She would never be tempted by streets paved with
gold.

Yet she, too, gave Hannah a hug, hard, swift, and embarrassed. "Write to us, *maidele,*" she murmured now as lovingly as though she spoke to one of her daughters. "Live Torah." And then—did she truly say it, or did Hannah only imagine? "Forgive me."

Forgive her for what? For not being Mama? For being an orphan girl, clumsy and awkward? For being as God had made her?

Hannah had no time to deal with these questions. A whistle screeched. Steam billowed out from under the waiting train like sooty, windblown curtains wreathing the eager wheels. Shy Sara, her baby a great lump of scarves in her arms, tore herself from her parents' embrace and bravely mounted the carriage steps. A hand reached down to help her. A hoarse voice barked out, "All aboard . . . aboard . . . abo-o-ard . . . ."

"Hannah! Hannah!" Sara called.

It was Aunt Yehudis who hugged Hannah last.

Her aunt's arms tight about her, Hannah stared up into the deeply seamed face that had so long watched over her, and she shivered with surprise. Aunt Yehudis had grown old. The thick, black hair escaping from beneath her *babushka* had turned gray.

"I—I will never see you again, Aunt Yehudis!"

"But you will think of me often, *maidele,* and I will think of you. Be a good girl. Be safe. When you are a great violinist, send me news."

A band was blaring loudly on the Antwerp wharf as the steamship *Astra* prepared to leave her moorings, but overhead the skies were leaden gray. Raindrops, like angry glass bees, glittered on the bells of the musicians' bright brass horns. The wet wind blew strong.

On the deck of the *Astra,* gained after so many weeks of delay and of travel, Hannah ducked under the elbows of the cheering, tightly packed crowd of grown-ups until she reached the ship's rail. There, she stared down.

Beneath her feet the *Astra* began to tremble. Soon a narrow ribbon of rain-pocked water separated the ship's side from the wharf.

Slowly the ribbon widened. Became a channel. In the distance the open roadstead beckoned ships from the inner harbor to the sea.

On the *Astra*'s crowded deck, the cheers of departure died away into silence. Faces grew grave. Hannah felt her heart rap hard against her breastbone.

Impulsively she ducked back under the thicket of elbows to find Sara. The young woman had seen nothing of the departure. Her face was pressed blindly into the bundle of scarves that held her baby. Her thin body trembled.

"You must not be afraid, Sara. I have heard people say that it will take us eighteen days to cross the ocean. Who would have guessed it would take so long? But in eighteen days, you will see your Jacob. Until then, the *Astra* will be our home. I think it will be a good one."

Despite Hannah's brave words, the steerage sleeping room to which the crewmen led them was most unhomelike. Deep in the ship, it was a big, airless space without portholes. Beds were stacked like boxes, floor to ceiling, wall to wall. People had to scuttle over each other to find their resting places. Tall and short, thin and round, young and old, they knelt and scrambled, dragging with them food and possessions needed for the crossing.

Hannah was thankful to be small. After she had followed Sara to reach her own canvas mattress, she discovered she could sit upright without bumping her head on the bottom of the bed above her. Then, after so much excitement, she was ravenous.

Gripping her arms over her stomach, she moaned, "Sara, Sara, I am starved!"

Her prayers, said, Sara broke off chunks of dark bread from one of the loaves wrapped in her shawl, and she sliced a big purple onion. Eyes streaming both from the onion and from her fright, she laid the crisp pungent rings out upon the bread.

Hannah ate eagerly. "You must eat, too, Sara," she admonished. "Aunt Yehudis would say we must both keep up our strength." The meal ended, she kissed the baby, gave Sara a hug for courage, and curled in a tight ball on her mattress. She had meant to watch over the other two and sing the poor, thin baby a lullaby, but, in fact, she was soon fast asleep.

Hannah wakened to terrible cries of panic. People were shouting out frantic questions. Those on the beds nearest the door had slid to their feet and were pressing desperately toward that exit.

They did not go far. From her bed Hannah could see them dimly, a great clot of bodies thrusting and struggling. A member of the ship's crew, back to the door, was trying to calm them, gesturing with head and arms, shouting a stream of strange words over and over.

Since the *Astra* was an English vessel, Hannah decided it must be English that the crewman spoke. But who could understand him? What did he say?

I will learn English tomorrow! Hannah promised herself.

Even without that language, she soon guessed the cause of alarm. The *Astra,* which had trembled so gently at the wharf in Antwerp, must now be out in the rough, open sea. For she was plunging wildly up and down, up and down.

Mixed with the voices of the terrified passengers were other, even more ominous sounds—a hoarse, distant horn and a faraway shrieking.

"That is the wind we hear." The explanations began to be passed from neighbor to neighbor in languages each could understand. "The wind is shrieking. . . . We are in the midst of a storm. The lowering sky over Antwerp and the ropes tied about the decks should have been a warning. God forbid the ship is too weak to carry us through such waves!"

For hours the *Astra* was a giant rocking horse, angrily, powerfully receiving the waves' attacks. With all the indignant groans of her strong timbers, she kept plunging. Up and down. Up and down.

Hannah grasped the rails at her bedside, pressed her feet against the bed's end, and held herself taut. Up and down. Up and down. Her head grew light with the motion. It was a kettle which might at any moment fly off.

By now the cries and questions of the passengers were silenced. Everyone was back in bed. Who could stand? Even the strongest men struggling to keep to their feet had been dashed against the wall.

The sounds in the big sleeping room soon became wordless groans. Such seasickness! The food that people had eaten earlier was wasted. A sick-sweet smell hung heavy over all.

Hannah threw her shawl across her face. She had never in her life felt so strange, but her head had not yet flown apart. *Her* supper was not yet wasted. "I—I think I shall be a good sailor. Aunt Yehudis would be proud." She reached a comforting hand to the next bed.

"Sara . . . Sara. . . ."

But poor Sara, limp beside her weakly wailing baby, could answer only with a moan. Carefully, Hannah took the baby into her arms.

In the continuing storm, the ship's bells marked the passing time, or so people whispered. But who could understand the bells' exact message or know if it was night or day?

Yet storms, like people, Hannah decided, must now and again be obliged to rest. Gradually, the wind quieted. The ship settled more steadily into the waves.

After a long while, the doors of the big room were thrown open. This time, members of the ship's crew came beckoning. Hannah lifted her head from her mattress to try to understand.

"We are to go on deck," the word ran round the close-packed space. "All of us are to go at once. They will clean our beds while we breathe fresh air. They say it will do us good."

Indeed, the fresh air was a bracing medicine. It streamed, clean and salty, into Hannah's nostrils as she reached the open deck. Her feverish cheeks cooled. Her head was its familiar self again, no longer a kettle lid threatening to blow off.

When she had helped settle Sara and the baby where they could rest against a great coil of rope, she herself went across the smoothly rolling deck. This time there was no barrier of tight-packed elbows. Few of the grown-ups were yet able to stand steadily. Only a half-dozen children played by the rail, jumping happily with the ship's motion.

Eagerly Hannah sucked in still more of the cool, reviving air, and then glanced toward her companions. A few steps away from her, a little girl with a scarf like purple butterfly wings tugged at the sleeve of a tall, blond boy who, Hannah decided, must be her brother.

"Can you see America, Eric?" the little one demanded in German.

"Of course not, *dummkopf*. Everyone knows that we will not see America for days and days. America is nearly three thousand miles away, a ninth of the distance around the earth."

The tall boy was showing off, Hannah thought. Yet what he said might well be true. She herself could see no sign of land. On all sides the ocean stretched to the horizon in billowing waves like coarse dark silk. Overhead the sky, like the water, was still heavy and gray.

"We will have more storm," the tall boy announced, this time obviously speaking over the little girl's head to Hannah. When he saw that she had noticed and understood his German, he went on boldly.

"I am Eric Stein. I am fourteen years old, and I know about storms from my papa, who has crossed the Atlantic before. My papa has already lived for five years in America, but he came back to Germany to get us. He did not want his family to face the dangers of travel alone.

"You must understand that my papa is a watchmaker, and we have a fine new house waiting for us, with a stained-glass window by the door. We could have traveled first class, not steerage, but we decided to save the money for furniture for our home."

Hannah thought she had never heard such a braggart, not even wild Muni in a rage. She stepped back quickly to Sara's side. The thin baby smiled at her coming.

Soon, however, Hannah discovered that, despite his self-importance, the tall boy was right. The storm had not ended. Doubly fierce and violent, it struck again that night when they were all settled back in their beds.

This time the plunging steerage became a kind of cauldron, threatening to throw bodies about like cord wood. Men and women used their shawls to tie themselves and their families to the bed rails. Tied so tightly against Sara and the baby, Hannah could scarcely breathe.

At last came the disaster.

A wave, so tremendous that it seemed the ocean itself must be emptied, struck the *Astra*'s side. Thunder rushed through the ship. From somewhere above deck, bells and horns sounded frantically. Whistles shrilled. Voices shouted. The very motion of the ship changed abruptly. She no longer plunged like a giant rocking horse but, like a wounded animal, lurched from side to side, her engines powerless and silenced.

After what seemed forever, word came to the steerage. It was not a wave, after all, that had struck the *Astra*. It was the prow of another vessel, a small cargo ship. In the darkness of the storm, the two had collided without warning. The force of that collision had damaged the *Astra*'s side. But the ship was strong and sturdy. Despite the accident, she was staying afloat in the angry waves.

When the storm winds had at last blown themselves out and the worst of the wreckage had been cleared away, the passengers were allowed to go up on deck once more. There, standing feebly upon uncertain feet or clinging anxiously to the rail, they stared at the world about the crippled *Astra*. They looked toward the far horizon, where sky and water closed together like the valves of a vast gray shell.

"We are scarcely started upon our journey to America." The tall boy, Eric Stein, had once again joined Hannah at the rail. "My papa has talked to the crewmen. They say the damage to the ship can be mended. We will not have to be towed back to port, as they feared. But the storm has already slowed us badly. We are only a few hundred miles off the coast of Ireland."

"Ireland?" This time Hannah was too curious to draw back from this self-assured boy. "What is Ireland?"

"It is an island. One of the British Isles. This means we have hardly left Europe behind us."

Hannah shook her head dubiously. After so much time? "Are you certain?"

"Look. I will make you a map." Eric knelt to draw an outline with his finger on the ship's damp deck. "Here is

Ireland, there England, Scotland, Wales. Back across the English Channel is Antwerp in Belgium, where we embarked, then Germany, and still farther east, Poland. You must have come that way. See, the map shows it all."

Hannah, kneeling down beside him, stared wonderingly. In Reb Doddl's school she had not learned such things.

"Show me my *shtetl,* Eric," she demanded. "Put my *shtetl* on the map, too."

But he shook his head.

"I am a Berliner. I know nothing of *shtetls."* Then, at the sight of her disappointed face, he said, "One thing I can teach you, which I have learned from my papa: I can teach you English. Would you like that?"

"Oh, yes, yes, I would like that very much. But I have not told you my name. I am Hannah. Hannah Eliashov."

"I think you will learn English quickly, Hannah. I can see you are not a *dummkopf* like my little sister. Nor always scared."

"With your sister you are not patient," Hannah told him firmly, although she could not help being pleased at his praise. "First, before my English lesson, Eric, draw me a map of America. Show me New York and Youngstown and Pittsburgh, Pennsylvania."

"We-ell," he said, grimacing lightly, "I will do what I can."

Meanwhile, the ship's carpenters had begun repairs on the damaged vessel. Their hammers pounded. The welders' torches crimsoned and added their own shrill, sizzling notes.

And the sea itself changed once again. It had been a

cauldron and then a cradle, gently rocking. Now it became a mirror, smooth as glass.

Gradually, that glass clouded. Fog wrapped around the *Astra,* pale gray, unmoving. No wind blew, not a breath. The world, which had previously stretched to the far horizon, shrank to the size of the ship herself.

A day of fog passed. . . . Hannah now knew how to tell the time from the sound of the ship's bells, whose meaning, along with her English lessons, Eric had taught her. . . . A night of fog passed. Another day and night. Impenetrable, silent.

"We are all dead spirits! God has sent us a shroud," Sara sobbed in her bed in the steerage.

"But I do not feel dead at all," Hannah declared.

And the next morning, a gentle rocking told her that she was right. The wind and waves must be rising. Surely the fog would lift.

Indeed, when she clambered eagerly up on deck, she found a bright sky and white, scudding clouds. It was at noontime, with Eric standing at the rail beside her, that she felt a fresh trembling go over the ship, a pulse like the beat of a giant heart.

"The engines!" Eric cried, as passengers rushed up on deck shouting with new-found strength, the men tossing their caps into the air. "We are once again on our way to America!"

America &

In her most astonishing dreams, Hannah had not foreseen the wonders of the great port of New York. The tall, guardian skyscrapers watching the thronged harbor with their many window eyes . . . the myriad vessels clanging and shrilling with bells and whistles . . . the fireboats glittering with brass and red paint . . . the small tugs like overgrown beetles nosing great transatlantic steamers to their docks . . . barges crowded with men, women, and children, tight-packed to the rail, moving from the shadow of those steamers toward Ellis Island . . . Ellis Island itself, its red brick immigration building rising with high, arching windows, as if it had just sprung from the water and now hovered upon the harbor lip.

This was the largest building in which Hannah had ever set foot. Only in Antwerp had she seen any building half so big. She and Sara went breathlessly in at the door, pressed on by the dark-clothed flow of immigrants and urged by uniformed officials who waved their arms, bawled out directions, and now and again gave a mighty shove.

Peering into the faces of the officials, she saw that these men had not the hard, blank eyes of the Tsar's soldiers at home. Yet, with the heat of the summer morning and the confusions of their task, they were growing red-faced and impatient.

"Do not worry, Sara," Hannah whispered. "I will understand when they speak to us. Eric has taught me English."

Arms locked together, the two, with the baby, mounted the broad stairs which rose before them. They had little choice of motion, since they were now pushed forward by those behind them, now halted by those above.

"We must remember to have our papers all ready," Hannah whispered again into Sara's ear. "Eric says the officials will ask whether our families in America are willing to receive us. We must show proof of that."

But the families, even those like Sara's Jacob, who lived in New York, could not receive them yet. That became clear as they reached the huge room at the top of the stairway. No waiting families were in sight, only barriers.

Throughout the arching, high-ceilinged hall, Hannah could see the lines of anxious-faced travelers, held fast within a network of metal railings. In tiny cages behind the railings, officials sat shuffling piles of papers, and doctors questioned, one by one, the immigrants who came before them.

"We must be careful to answer every question just as we answered the officials in Warsaw," Hannah admonished one last time. "Eric says we must be careful not to make the least change, or they will think we are dishonest."

"But I—I cannot remember what I said. I cannot remember my own p-papa's name!" Sara stammered, and when at last it was her turn to answer the first questions, she paled and trembled so that no words came from her lips.

Hannah had opened her mouth to speak for them both,

when all at once there was a scuffle in the line behind her.

"Someone has fainted!"

"No wonder! Such a crowd! Such heat!" an old woman cried plaintively.

Children began to wail. Some people tried to push forward to help the fallen one, while others pushed them back. "Make breathing space!" Still others jostled their neighbors to make sure that they did not lose their places in line.

The official who had been facing Sara pushed his cap back from his perspiring forehead and muttered angrily. Then, without further questions, he shoved Sara's and Hannah's papers back across the table and hurried away through the crowd. "Order! We must have order!" he bawled.

But it was not, after all, the harried officials of whom one had to be afraid the most. It was the nurses, the doctors.

Eric had had no need to tell Hannah of that danger. All the way across the Atlantic, passengers had whispered fearfully, "The doctors could send us back. For sickness of the eyes, for a hundred reasons. It has happened many times."

"Put your clothing there, upon the hook," a stern-faced nurse directed, folding her hands tight against her stomach as though she dared not touch their soiled and well-worn garments.

When Hannah had taken off her thick, sweaty stockings and her stained jumper and blouse, she felt the blood rushing hotly to her cheeks. With lowered eyes, she saw that she was much thinned by the journey. Sara must never before have looked so frail, and, as for the baby, despite his two years he seemed no bigger than a doll unwrapped from his bundle of sour-smelling shawls.

Yet it was the baby who smiled and sat up happily as the heavy layers dropped away from him. Shy and fretful at the beginning of their travels, the little boy had by now lived so much among strangers that he was no longer afraid.

"Tell your husband for me that he will have to fatten his family if he does not want them to fly away in the first high wind. But I find no sickness. Welcome to America," the doctor said to Sara with gruff kindliness when his examination of eyes, ears, throats, and chests was at last complete.

Like sunlight upon water, a sheen of joy shimmered on Sara's thin cheeks. She threw her arms passionately about Hannah.

"Without you, I would never have had the courage to reach this day," she cried. "My Jacob will be waiting for us beyond that tall gate. He will thank you, *maidele*. He will care for you as for his own. God be praised."

Throughout the long journey, Sara had never spoken so many words all at once. More surprising words were to come.

In the crowd thrusting toward the exit gate, the Stein family suddenly appeared. Eric's papa, who had gone through Ellis Island before, knew how to force a path, Hannah saw. With one hand he propelled his wife forward and with the other, his daughter. He shouted over his shoulder to his son.

"Stay close behind us, Eric! Do not hang back! Hurry!"

But Eric had caught a glimpse of Hannah's bright red hair. He hesitated and then pushed his way toward her.

"Hannah, we must see each other in America!"

"How shall we do that, Eric?"

To her astonishment, he shook his head. "How to tell?"

"You can give me your address."

"I have no address."

"Surely there is an address for the fine house with the stained-glass window by the door?"

At her question, all Eric's bold confidence seemed to slip away. He returned her gaze, shamefaced.

"There is no house. That was only Papa's story. He confessed to us last night. He had spoken of a house because he feared Mama would not leave Germany without that promise. I think that he was right.

"Tonight we are going to a hotel. It will be a fine hotel, of course, not an immigrant hostel. Papa says so. We will be very comfortable."

Then, as abruptly as he had appeared, the boy was vanishing. From somewhere in the crowd surging toward the gate, his papa's voice commanded, *"Eric, come with us!"*

"I have already told you. I will be with Rachel, Moishe Kopsofsky's Rachel, in Pittsburgh, Pennsylvania," Hannah called.

"I will find you there!"

Hannah saw the quick lift of his cap, and then he was gone altogether. Many bodies hid him. There was a fresh surge in the crowd, and she could see nothing, for her nose was pressed suffocatingly into the dark, steamy garments of a stranger. Even Sara, though they had tried so hard to cling to each others' arms, was forced away beyond her touch.

And suddenly, above the confusion of bodies and cries, a young man's voice sounded, frantic with relief and delight.

"Sara! My Sara! Do you see me?"

"Jacob! Jacob!"

Hannah managed to free her face from her neighbor's garment in time to see Sara, with a speed and strength which seemed impossible for her, throw herself forward through the crowd.

"Let me pass! I am coming to my husband!"

In another moment, mother and child were swallowed up, out of sight.

And now, for the first time since she had left the *shtetl,* panic swept Hannah. She threw herself about, arms flailing, a desperate whirligig struggling to make a space.

"With those nearsighted eyes, Sara will never see me from a distance," she sobbed to herself. "Her Jacob does not know me. They can't force their way back from the gate to look. They may have forgotten me altogether. And if I go forward with this crowd, I will be swept away. How shall I ever find myself?"

As that last question seared her throat, a hand closed beneath her armpit. Powerless to resist, she felt herself half-lifted, half-pulled away between angry, protesting people.

"The child has kicked me! She is having a tantrum! What a disgrace!"

"No, no, not a tantrum. Not a disgrace." Above her head, a firm voice speaking in Yiddish contradicted the others, a voice which seemed somehow to go with the hand that held her. "Make way for us, please. It is plain that the little girl is lost."

Mercifully, at last a space seemed to open. Free of the swaying, pressing barrier of dark-clad bodies, Hannah lifted her eyes. She caught her breath in relief. The man who bent above her was a stranger, it was true, but he wore a dark suit and a blue uniform cap with four Hebrew letters embroidered in gold across it. She did not know what words the letters stood for, but they looked familiar and comforting.

"Trust me. I am your friend. I come from the Hebrew Immigration Aid Society," the man told her. "Was I right? You are lost?"

"Oh, yes. Please do not go away." Now it was she who held tightly to his sleeve. "I am Hannah Eliashov, on my way to my sister Rachel—Moishe Kopsofsky's Rachel—in Pittsburgh, Pennsylvania. She is expecting me to come to her. Can you help me find the way?"

"Rachel Kopsofsky? Pittsburgh? I am glad to hear you say that someone is waiting for you. No doubt we will have a message." The man smiled in relief. "So many are lost altogether. They should have sent you to my office at once."

"Someone fainted in the line when we came to the first desk in the hall," Hannah remembered. "The official hurried away to help. He must have forgotten me."

"No matter now. Come. Surely, somewhere in my office we will find a letter."

And indeed it was so. In the cluttered room to which he led the way, the man shuffled through a great pile of papers. As Hannah watched breathlessly, he drew out an envelope addressed in Rachel's familiar, cramped hand.

"Your sister has sent directions and a railroad ticket," he exclaimed, wiping his damp cheeks with a great white handkerchief. "We do not have to worry about you, God be praised. But you have a day-long trip before you. Before you board the train, you must have food and a good night's rest. I will bring a lady to take you to the Aid Society hostel. She will also send a telegram to your sister, telling her that you are well."

Hannah remembered then that she was Papa's and Mama's daughter, who had panicked for a moment but who did not forget her manners for long.

She bowed and said in English, so that he would know she had the words, "Good-bye, and thank you. You are very kind."

With a quick grin, he ruffled her red hair.

"You will find your way in America, little carrot-top. I have no doubt of that."

Indeed, although she herself had no doubt, she ate no supper that night at the hostel and did not sleep at all. Excitement kept her staring, wide-eyed, into the darkness. Even in her clean, soft bed, she tossed hour after hour.

The next morning, she was waiting early as the Aid Society lady who had guided her yesterday came bustling to the hostel door.

"We have had a call from your friends, Sara and Jacob. They thought we might have found you. They were frantic about you," the lady said. "You wish to go to them?"

"No, I must go to Rachel. Tell them not to worry. I am safe."

The lady nodded.

"You have eaten a good breakfast, Hannah?"

"No, I could not."

"You will be hungry."

"*No!* We must go to the railroad station. At once."

She was a veteran of trains now. She had known them in Poland, Germany, and Belgium. She must be on time.

"I have one surprise before we go." The lady delayed a last moment, slipping a cardboard box from beneath her arm. "Here is a present from the Aid Society to a brave girl."

In the box which Hannah opened were a new blue tam and a matching jumper of the same soft, shiny material.

"So that you will be beautiful when you reach your sister, Hannah. Remember, though, that you have a long journey before you see her. You will travel all day long. You will get off the train only when the conductor tells you that you have reached Pittsburgh.

"Along the way, you will not talk to strangers. America is a great country. Most of its people are good and kind. *But you must not talk to strangers.*"

Hannah nodded. "It is the same in Europe. Aunt Yehudis told me so. Papa, also. They said there are dangers, though I did not see them. But in Europe, no one gave me such a beautiful blue jumper and tam. I must put them on at once. And then, can we go to the train?"

Flags fluttered in the streets of New York that warm summer morning. Bunting with red, white, and blue stripes and bright circlets of blue stars hung above windows and doorways. Somewhere in the distance a band was playing. Perhaps, Hannah thought, New York was always decorated, celebrating. The distant band accented the excited pounding of her heart.

In the station, the train was waiting. Her companion explained matters at much length in English to the conductor. Though she need not have. I can explain for myself, Hannah thought, embarrassed.

She smiled up at the conductor in apology for the lady's anxious flow of words. Unexpectedly, the conductor winked back at her.

"Hop aboard, bluebird," he commanded. Hannah had never seen a bluebird in the *shtetl,* but, thanks to her fine new clothes, she had now been given a far more glamorous nickname than "carrot-top."

All that day, she sat proudly upright by her coach window, watching America glide past. The great city of Philadelphia, with its countless houses . . . the farmlands, green, silken, with their crops rising sturdily from the earth . . . the wide rivers . . . the mountains, their thickly wooded slopes sometimes rising up steeply past the coach window, sometimes falling away from the rails.

Now and again, the conductor would come through the car calling out names that Hannah had never heard before— she had not guessed there were so many towns in this Pennsylvania—and the train would stop. Passengers would climb off and on.

In time, the train slowed to yet another longer stop, and the conductor came into the car with a leather bag under his arm. He paused beside Hannah. "I get off here, bluebird," he told her. "We have a change of crew. A new conductor will go on to Pittsburgh. I have told him to look after you. He can't miss you. We don't have such passengers every day."

She did not understand all his English, but enough of it. Certainly, she understood his last friendly wink, his smile.

"Though I wish that you did not have to go away, I will be safe. Thank you."

Now, as she swallowed the uneasiness she felt at the sight of his broad, retreating back, she prepared for many more hours.

Once, the tracks made such an enormous horseshoe about the edge of a great ridge that Hannah, craning her neck, could see the train flipping its tail of coaches along the far side of the curve. After the first startled glance, she was not truly astonished. In America anything could happen.

Morning had long since ended. Noontime was gone. The sun moved westward, and the train raced after its retreating light.

It was hot in the coach. Up and down the aisle, people curled up wearily on the hard, straight seats and slept. Still Hannah did not close her eyes. Again and again she smoothed her new blue jumper, readjusted the tam pulled down over her tangled red curls. She could not risk spoiling such fine clothes or failing to impress Rachel with her grandeur.

Then, at last, when they had come to the day's end—was it the world's end, also—she felt the train begin one last time to jolt and slow. Above the sound of the train's braking, the conductor called out, *"Pittsburgh."* He came down the aisle, repeating his call. As he reached Hannah's side, he bent down toward her.

"Your station, little girl. Do you need—"

Before he could embarrass her with his help, she seized

up her bag and the crumpled shawl that had served her as a wrap until this morning. Eagerly, she rushed along the aisle and jumped down the coach steps so quickly that she nearly fell.

No matter! She would be falling into Rachel's arms!

But that did not happen, after all. Her sister was not standing at the foot of the coach steps. Hannah did not find her in the huge, murky waiting room either. There she saw only strange faces.

Gradually weariness numbed her, numbed even her fear and surprise. She moved toward a long wooden bench in a far corner and sank down upon it, suddenly so hungry that her stomach was one dull throb. She pulled a loaf of bread from the bundle she had made of her shawl. The Aid Society lady had given her the loaf many hours ago, but she had been unable to swallow a crumb. Now she ate ravenously.

As the last lumps slipped down her throat, she found herself drowsily remembering that she had not closed her eyes since yesterday morning, when she had left the *Astra.* Already half-asleep, she folded her familiar, salt-smelling shawl into a pillow and laid her head upon it. In an instant, her eyelids flew tight shut.

When she wakened, she thought at first that she was in a dream world. A gentle hand shook her shoulder, and a young woman who looked remarkably like Mama was bending over her. Tears streamed down the lovely, dark face.

They were real tears, not fancies. All at once she felt them falling upon her own cheeks.

"Oh, Hannah! You are here, Hannah! I have been so

frightened. When Moishe came to the station for you, there was a parade blocking his way in the street. He was fifteen minutes late. When he learned that the train had gone on and he could not find you, he came home in despair.

"Moishe was looking for a tiny girl in *shtetl* clothes, but you have grown so, you are wearing such a lovely jumper. And the blue tam covers all your red hair. I myself scarcely know you. Oh, you are beautiful, *liebchen*! We must have a picture taken of you very soon."

"You are beautiful, also," Hannah breathed as Rachel held her tight.

They could not cling to each other for long, however.

"We must go home to the others at once. Moishe and Leibel and the baby, Uri, are all waiting for you. We have talked of nothing but our Hannah for weeks. Quick. Give me your bag."

Soon they were outside the big station, where the dusky evening air hung warm and soft. Rachel led the way swiftly up a steep, littered street, around one corner and then another, where plain, red brick houses pressed friendly, sooty faces close to narrow sidewalks. Everywhere, people were walking, laughing, arguing, calling to each other in Yiddish. And here, as in New York, buntings hung over street corners and buildings. Red, white, and blue flags fluttered. Rosettes billowed in the breeze.

Hannah shook her head dizzily. Perhaps streets were always decorated in America. Perhaps people always had time to talk and laugh. She had no chance to ask. Rachel was so busy, pausing every now and again to hug her and then bustling on rapidly, all the while asking questions and not stopping for answers. She poured out her own story of Moishe and their little ones and their home on the third story of a house on the Hill, where they could look down on Pittsburgh's rivers.

With so much hurry and excitement, Hannah's head spun more and more rapidly.

It was when they finally stopped beside a lighted doorway—"This is home, *maidele*!"—that she heard a sudden rush of sound. A long stem of light shot up into the sky overhead. At its highest tip, a flower of light unfolded, petals flashing out all blue and rose and red. A second rush of sound followed, and beyond the first flower another opened against the darkening sky.

Hannah stared, speechless.

What is it, Rachel? Am I dreaming, after all?

She had no need to ask the questions aloud. Her sister was laughing softly.

"These are fireworks, *maidele*. I'm sure you've never seen them before. Fireworks for the holiday."

"Holiday?"

"You did not know? It is the Fourth of July."

"The Fourth of July?"

"The birthday of the United States. I will tell you that story later. Now you must come inside. The others will be wondering what has become of us."

Dazzled and panting, Hannah followed Rachel into a narrow, lighted hallway and up steep stairs to a small, fragrant kitchen where Moishe stood and, at the sight of her, reached out his powerful arms. In spite of her nearly eleven years and the dignity of her new blue jumper and tam, he swung her up high.

"You have come just in time, little sister," he teased her. "If you had grown for another year, it is *you* who would have had to lift *me.*"

Clearly Moishe, with his broad, tanned face, his thick golden hair, and laughing eyes, had not changed in America. He was the Moishe Kopsofsky she knew well.

It was the children who were strangers—thin, shy-eyed Leibel in a shiny wooden high chair and Uri, the fat, wobbly-chinned baby in his crib.

"Our Leibel grows more and more like his uncle every day," Rachel said, smiling proudly. "Already he watches over his baby brother. He runs errands for his mama and papa like a little man."

Hannah hugged the children. They were not so beautiful as Mashka and Eidel at home in the *shtetl,* she thought, but she would learn to love them soon. Lifting her face from their small ones, she heard another sound. Music!

Rachel and Moishe turned triumphantly toward the closed door at the far side of the kitchen.

"Another surprise, *maidele* !"

The notes were clear, high, and sweet. They were the notes of a mazurka played upon a violin. The mazurka that she had loved so long.

Rachel and Moishe pointed and gestured.

"Open the door, Hannah."

Before she could obey, the music ended and the door was

flung open from the other side. Then it was Aaron who came rushing to her, Aaron whose arms held her tight.

"You must forgive me for not meeting you at the station, *maidele.*"

"I do! I do, Aaron. Oh, but you look so handsome. You are wearing such a fine suit. You—"

"All this was not just to surprise you," Rachel interrupted. "Aaron is dressed splendidly because he played at his first concert this afternoon. Is he not wonderful, Hannah? He has been in Pittsburgh such a short time, and already he plays in a fine string quartet."

"And earns real money," added Moishe, beaming.

But Hannah was staring now beyond Aaron into the room he had left. There, upon a table, lay the violin Mama had purchased so long ago in the *shtetl*! She would have known it anywhere.

Her thoughts flew back to the interrupted *seder* and the night the violin had vanished.

"Oh, Aaron," she cried, "then you *did* know him—the poor man, Reb Abba, who came to our house that Sabbath? You yourself were hidden not far from the *shtetl*?"

"Yes, *maidele.* You can't think how I longed to see you all, but I dared not visit. I would have put myself and you, also, in such danger. So I sent Reb Abba to bring me news. He also brought me my life—my violin."

"I was right, then! Reb Abba was not Leah's papa. He was not what our papa thought him. He was not a common thief."

At those words, Aaron hesitated. A shadow fell over his

handsome face. For an instant, Hannah felt a cold twist of warning. Unlike Moishe, her brother had changed.

But perhaps, after all, a prince must hold himself aloof.

"A thief?" Aaron repeated slowly. "Truth to tell, *maidele,* I was never certain about that. Reb Abba was a strange man. He had been out of the world so long that at first he had no sense of the value of things. Once he realized the value of the violin, I feared he would take it. That was why I left him."

"You left him?"

"Yes. One moonless night, on a farm near the Polish border, we were sleeping together in a haystack. He was a sound sleeper, Reb Abba. And tired after so many weeks of flight. I crept away in the darkness with my violin. He never found me."

"But Reb Abba helped you escape from the Tsar's army!"

Aaron nodded.

"He helped me escape, yes. He could not help me reach my goal. He would only have hindered that. I could not trust him. He was not as strong as I, and not clever. He would have remained a pauper in England."

"In England?" Hannah remembered the map that Eric had drawn for her on the *Astra*'s wet deck. "That was not so far away."

Once again, Aaron nodded.

"Although I could not hope to pay my way to America at once, I could reach England easily. I played my violin upon street corners and earned money for the passage."

"And the rest of the story is most amazing," Rachel

interrupted once again, impatient, Hannah thought, with all these questions and answers. "Aaron has not told you the rest. In London, he went into a small music shop to buy violin strings, and there, behind the counter, he found Muni."

"Muni?"

"Yes. Was that not a miracle?"

"Then Muni is here, too? Another surprise?"

"No." Aaron took up his tale. "Our Muni has changed greatly, Hannah. You would hardly know him. He was turned away from Ellis Island and put on a ship going back across the Atlantic to Liverpool. On the ship, he met an older man who had also been refused. Muni had trachoma, a sickness of the eyes which has long since mended, but the other has a sickness in the lungs which nothing will cure. Muni says he owes his life to his friend and will not leave him. He will work for him in the music shop as long as the man is alive."

"Then our brother may never come to America?"

Aaron bowed gravely.

"That is true, little one. Muni has sent me instead."

Finally Rachel could no longer restrain her impatience. She rushed across the kitchen to her stove and lifted kettle lids, one after the other, so that the fragrance of hot foods was wafted out into the room.

"Enough of stories," she cried. "We will have time for them later. We must feast before we go to the Fourth of July celebration. I tell you, I have cooked for days."

And it was Rachel, beside herself with pride and excitement, who did the rest of the talking as the family crowded around the kitchen table to enjoy her bounty.

"You are not forgotten, Leibel, my son. Wait another moment and you will have a big slice of bread. . . . No more screaming, Uri, my treasure. I will serve you as soon as I can. Others are waiting, too. . . ." And to Hannah, with that smile so like Mama's, she said, "You must know that you will soon see your other brother, *maidele*. Chaim is coming from Youngstown to visit you and to introduce his Miriam. Chaim never ceased to mourn Leibel. For a long time, he would not come to us or write to us at all. The thought of seeing us wakened memories he could not bear. But at last he has found himself a sweetheart. She is making him happy. His heart is at peace, God be praised."

With all her busy chatter, Rachel had timed matters well.

The family feast was ending when, from outside the kitchen window, there came a fresh rush of sound, a fresh dazzle of light. Against the dark sky, a fountain of colors danced and sprayed.

"For the Fourth of July!" exclaimed Moishe. "More fireworks. There is to be a great display. Come. We must all go outside to watch." He seized Leibel from his high chair. Rachel gathered Uri from his crib. Aaron himself lifted Hannah into his strong arms. With her head nestled against his shoulder, she was carried down the steep apartment stairs.

On the hillside in the darkness, other people were arriving, welcoming Rachel, welcoming Moishe, welcoming all their neighbors, and exclaiming at each new burst of light.

The fireworks were now in full display. Golden fountains leaped skyward. Flowers, blue, red, green, and dazzling white, shot up swiftly, uncurling on magical stems. Rockets zoomed in glittering balls of flame. Small Leibel clapped his hands fearfully to his ears at each explosion and burrowed his face into his papa's broad chest, but bold Uri in Rachel's arms laughed and pointed with delight. After the fountains, flowers, rockets, came, at last, the flag.

"It is Old Glory!" people cheered.

Hannah stared up at the shining image, the red and white stripes, the stars bright on their blue field. The flag swayed gently, as if wind-touched. For a long moment it hung there. Then, in brilliant splinters of colored light, it divided and fell earthward. On the hillside, people drew, as if on a single breath, a great, satisfied sigh.

At that moment, Hannah pressed her lips impulsively against her brother's ear.

"In America, anything can happen, Aaron, anything! So we must begin my violin lessons tonight," she whispered. "I have dreamed of them, I have waited for them so long."

And then came the moment which was to change her life forever. In one instant, she had been a joyous, wide-eyed child beneath a sparkling holiday sky. In the next, she felt like a grain of cold, gray sand at the center of a stone.

For, even as she stopped speaking, she felt Aaron's body stiffen, his spirit withdraw. He did not speak for a long moment. When he did, his voice seemed to come from some far dream of his own.

"You must not talk nonsense, *maidele*. Let me tell you my good news. I didn't want to overshadow the excitement of your coming, so I said nothing at supper, but all the family must know soon. Our stringed quartet is moving to New York at the end of July. Already we have a half-dozen concert engagements there, and soon we will have more bookings. With that experience, and lessons from a fine New York teacher—for I shall be able to afford lessons now—I shall be on my way to a great career. Oh, Mama would be happy! Somehow, tonight I think she knows!"

"I could go to New York with you, Aaron. I could take care of you." Hannah's desperate plea did not seem to reach his ears. Perhaps she had not had the courage to speak aloud. They had not, after all, let her take care of Papa in the safe, familiar world of the *shtetl*. How should she take care of her brother in the huge, high city which she had left this morning —Fourth of July morning—could it have been a hundred years ago?

"The violin, Aaron?" she managed to force out the words. "You will take the violin with you?"

"What a question, little one! Shall I play on a broomstick in New York?" Aaron gave a hearty laugh. "Oh, someday, when I am rich, I shall buy myself a Guarneri or a Stradivarius, but as a starter my old instrument will do well enough. For a violin made by a poor *shtetl* fiddle maker, it has a surprisingly good tone."

It sings! It sings! How could Aaron speak so? An indignant pain coursed through Hannah's body. "Wh-when you have your Strad—"

"Stradivarius, *maidele.* Haven't you heard the name of the finest instruments ever made?"

"When you have bought your Stradivarius, Aaron, will you send the old violin to me?"

"To you?" For the merest instant, she thought he looked questioningly toward her in the darkness, thought he had heard the anguish in her voice. She was, after all, to be saved. But no! With another laugh, shorter and dryer, he slipped her down from his shoulder onto the hard earth.

"It will not be tomorrow, *maidele*. I can tell you that. I will not earn so much money so easily. But, yes, someday I will send you the violin. For now it is my bridge, my life."

Part Three

The Gift ✒

"And that was the very last of the tapes," Becka declared in the harsh spring light of Bobe's nursing-home bedroom. "I have heard them all, to the end. I listened even when Patrick and Judith thought I was sleeping and not understanding anything at all. I was *living* with you, Bobe! I was living your story, but you did not tell everything. You must tell me the rest. You cannot keep quiet any longer. Aaron never did send the violin, did he? He did not keep his promise?"

"Oh, yes, he kept his promise." The old woman's chin bobbed down to her chest and up again. The fierce eyes flickered as though the mind behind them had once again been stabbed to life. "Yes, he sent me the violin, but I put it away long ago."

"You put it away?"

"In the attic at home. It was only a poor *shtetl* fiddle, after all."

"In the *attic*? Why, then, it was your violin I saw that night, Bobe! Why did you never play it?"

"It came too late, girl. By the time Aaron sent it to me, I had long since gone to work with my brother Chaim in the Youngstown shirt factory. The machines there were not easy for me—I could not keep my mind on them. For months, I thought only of music, like Papa dreaming of the Talmud as he wove prayer shawls. One day, I made a wrong turn of the machine wheel and drove the needle through the index finger of my left hand. By bad luck, the bone was broken, the nerves affected, and the doctor was a hack.

"When you were very small, girl, you used to ask me why my hand was crippled, why I always tried to hide it from you. I thought it was too cruel a story to tell a child, but you see now why I never afterward touched an instrument. If I could not play beautifully, I did not want to play at all."

"Then—then—" Becka drew in a deep, sharp breath—"you have never heard your violin since that day you came to Pittsburgh, Bobe?"

"No, never. Never since that day." This time, the old head swayed sideways, ever so little, upon the pillow. The weary eyes shut. The voice trailed away in a sigh. "It was all so long ago, girl. Everyone is gone. All the Eliashovs. Papa, Mama, Aunt Yehudis, Aaron, stricken too young on a concert tour in Australia, Rachel, Chaim, Leibel, Muni. Leah, too. She died trying to give birth to the new son she had promised Papa. Even my beautiful baby sisters have gone, disappeared into those awful ovens of the Germans. Here in America, the Eliashov children and grandchildren have scattered. To Wyoming, California, Maine. The violin doesn't matter to me any longer. It doesn't matter, after all."

"But it *does* matter to her! Oh, I know it matters very much!" Becka exclaimed that night at the dinner table. "Bobe stopped talking—it had been all in English this time, you know—and shut her eyes, as if she were drifting away from me. But her eyes were not shut-shut. She was still *with* me, and aching. I was sure of that. I leaned over her to look. Her lips trembled. Big tears slid down her cheeks. I tell you, Judith, you have got to let me go back and visit her again."

"But you know what Dr. Cohn prescribed, Becka. A month of complete quiet for you, and I've already disobeyed him by letting you pay that one visit, since you wanted it so much."

"Quiet! There's no place quieter than Bobe's room. Dr. Cohn knows that himself."

"Still, he said a month. One month, Becka." But Judith was wavering. Pleadingly, Becka caught her hand.

"A month might be too long. Don't you understand that? A week could be too long. I could see how feeble she is, and how—well, how unsatisfied. I am going back tomorrow. You must take me. And I'm going with the violin."

As if spotlighted by the morning sun, the old woman lay so small and stiff and still amid crisp, white sheets that when Becka first stepped to the bedside, her own heart came close to stopping.

"Bobe, Bobe, do you see what I have brought for you?" she whispered slowly, hopelessly.

To her relief, the body twitched beneath the covers, the eyes opened. Something sprang to life behind them abruptly, like a candle being lit.

"Do I see? Of course, I see. You have brought my

violin," the old woman snapped. "What do you intend to have
me do with it, girl? Suppose you tell me that."

Becka pressed her lips tight together.

"I want you to sing the mazurka for me, Bobe."

"The mazurka?"

"The one Aaron played when you were a little girl in
the *shtetl*. I want to play it, too. Now. This morning."

"That shouldn't be hard. I used to hum it to your mother
when she was a baby, though I suppose she has forgotten.
Well, let us give it a try. If you keep your wits about you,
we can't come out too badly."

And indeed, they did not. The notes came from Bobe's
dry lips, cracked and harsh, but true as a pitch pipe. Becka
played them back, at first tentatively, and then in a satisfying
rush of sound. The melody circled the narrow white room like
a Catherine wheel, ever higher and brighter, till at last it
stopped as if on some shining hilltop.

"Beautiful, girl, beautiful!" Bobe gasped.

"But it was you who should have played it," Becka said
with a frown.

"I could never have done so well."

"You did not have a chance! Oh, Bobe, I could cry for
you."

"No, you must not do that. You must not waste your
pity on me, girl. I've had a good life.

"Oh, without the violin, I was miserable for my first
years in America, so homesick for Papa and Aunt Yehudis
and the twins and Leah, too, so homesick for the *shtetl*. I
thought I had left even God behind. I would gladly have

gone back across the ocean if I had had money for the ticket. I was too proud to write to Papa and Aunt Yehudis about my loneliness. One day when I was thirteen, I did run away, though Rachel never knew. I packed all my things in my old suitcase and went down to the railroad station. I was sure I would find a way to board the train when nobody was looking. I meant to stow away on a steamship when I reached New York. The conductor caught me on the steps— they were always so high, those train steps. He gave me a dreadful shaking and scolding and told me that, if I tried to do that again, he'd put me in jail where none of my family could ever find me. He was only trying to frighten me, of course.

"Soon after that, I went out to work in Youngstown, as I've told you, joined the garment workers' union, and made new friends. In time, Eric found me there. Eric had promised that he would see me again in the New World. He came looking for me at Rachel's in Pittsburgh and then in Youngstown.

"He had not had an easy time in the years we had been apart. His mama had never forgiven his papa for deceiving her about his prospects in America, and his papa had never got the good job he hoped for. But I could see that Eric was as clever as I thought him on the *Astra,* and his character had improved a great deal with all his troubles. So we were married, set up our jewelry business in Pittsburgh, and did so well that before long, we bought the house on St. James Place. It wasn't in a Jewish neighborhood, since Eric did not care about that. Eric was never interested in keeping up old ties, old ways. What he loved was the beautiful stained-glass fanlight above our door. Soon after we moved, I bore your grandmother, Rebecca. Such a lovely, delicate child. Who would have thought that a woman like me—small, and tough as a horse —would have only one, thin little girl, who couldn't lift a violin to her shoulder for half an hour at a sitting and who wouldn't live long enough, much as we loved her, to raise her own daughter? Who'd have thought that *that* child, so strong and ambitious, would take up such a foolish instrument as the harp? All gilt and glitter, with those showers of notes which make you feel someone has poured diamonds down your spine, then say nothing else to you. Nothing at all. Of course, you must not repeat that to Judith. . . ."

With the last words, Bobe drifted into silence, and Becka thought that she was falling asleep or would lapse into Yiddish and never come to the end of her tale. In a little while, however, she raised her chin, reopened her eyes, and reached out one clawlike little hand. It was the left hand with the misshapen finger, and she did not seem to realize that she was no longer hiding it. Perhaps she did not care. She slipped it boldly into Becka's.

"I say again—and you must believe me, girl—I've had a good life. Eric was always kind to me. When we could see that we were not going to have a large family, he took me into the store to work with him. Soon I was a better buyer than he was, and I loved the jewelry. I never wore any of the splendid pieces. I was a *shtetl* child with a crippled finger, after all. But I got much happiness from handling the gems and selling them to the beautiful ladies who showed them off so well. For more years than you could count, everybody in Pittsburgh came downtown to the Golden Triangle to Stein's Jewelers for diamonds and pearls.

"Then, when he was only fifty, Eric died. Your grandmother Rebecca had married David Berkowitz, a brilliant young lawyer who had no interest in business. When I could no longer manage the store, it was sold. I think it goes on still. I—I can't remember the name of the new owners. Everything new is—is blurry, girl. Blurry. I'm sorry. Only the old things are clear."

"No, that's not true. *I* am clear to you, Bobe. And my music. I am certain of that. Oh, you must come back home to us now. Where we can take care of you. Where I can play to you every day."

Bobe blinked owlishly.

"I am very well cared for here, thank you, girl. The nurses are kind. Dr. Cohn checks on me every day with a phone call or a visit. The rabbi comes every week. And the ladies from temple come, too—although, of course, they're all so young, in their fifties and sixties, that I hardly recognize them anymore. Best of all, I don't complicate your parents' lives."

"But, Bobe—"

"Let me finish, girl. Without the problem of caring for me and pleasing me, Patrick and Judith might have more time for each other, grow closer together, and come to feel that the house on St. James Place is *theirs*. It was because of that hope that I put on such a shocking show—forced them to send me here in the first place, you know."

"No, no, we didn't know! I thought you didn't like us, Bobe."

"Nonsense. I love you all dearly. . . . Anyhow, it turns out that none of you will be at home this summer, and I'm not strong enough to stay there alone."

"None of us will be there?"

During the days since Becka's fall, with her parents anxiously watching over her, she had blotted out any thought of the summer. Now that memory came back, startling and clear. Judith would be in Europe on her concert tour, Patrick with Marcy. Neither of them had spoken a word about changing those plans.

"None of us? Oh, Bobe, I mean to stay—"

The old woman's hand slipped out of hers, and the misshapen finger waggled reprovingly.

"I should hope you have been well enough brought up not to disobey your Bobe. I should hope you will do what she tells you to do."

"But you haven't told me!"

"Then I shall do it now. No matter what your parents decide for themselves, you are to be your own person, girl. You are to go to Tanglewood and practice every day till your poor body aches and your head spins, so that in time you can become a great musician. For you have the gift, girl. The true gift. It is your Bobe who says so, and she knows."

Becka laid her cheek against the old woman's and cried wordlessly, until her tears would no longer flow. Then the stern voice softened for a moment.

"You may be asking yourself, girl, 'What right has Bobe

to ask me to live her life for her, to fulfill *her* dream, the dream of those who have gone before?' It is a fair question. If you do not *want* to go to Tanglewood, if you do not want to be a musician, after all—"

Becka put a hand across the thin lips and pressed them gently shut. For a moment she stared deep into Bobe's eyes and was not surprised to find a new-born radiance. She knew that her own eyes must be shining. Everything about her must be shining.

"Hush, Bobe. Hush. Of course, I want to go to Tanglewood. I want to be the best violinist I could ever be. For your sake. For all the Eliashovs. And because," she concluded, despite her yearning for Patrick and Judith, despite the tangle of the unknown years ahead, "I could not dream of doing anything else with my life."

About the Author

MARGERY EVERNDEN spent her first twelve years in Okeechobee, Florida, where, taught by her mother, she devoted a great deal of time to reading, playing the piano, directing her four younger brothers and sisters in family plays and circuses, and, of course, to writing. When her family moved to California, she pursued a more traditional school life, eventually receiving a bachelor's degree from the University of California at Berkeley and a master's degree from the University of Pittsburgh. When her three children were in their teens, she began teaching in the English Department at the University of Pittsburgh while continuing her freelance writing career. Currently an enthusiastic and popular professor, Ms. Evernden and her husband, Earl Gulbransen, reside in Pittsburgh.